DATE DUE

THE
WILD BREED

Center Point
Large Print

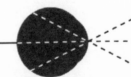

**This Large Print Book carries the
Seal of Approval of N.A.V.H.**

THE
WILD BREED

Roe Richmond

CENTER POINT LARGE PRINT
THORNDIKE, MAINE

This Center Point Large Print edition
is published in the year 2013 by arrangement with
Golden West Literary Agency.

The text of this Large Print edition is unabridged.
In other aspects, this book may vary
from the original edition.
Printed in the United States of America
on permanent paper.
Set in 16-point Times New Roman type.

ISBN: 978-1-61173-729-5

Library of Congress Cataloging-in-Publication Data

Richmond, Roe.
The wild breed / Roe Richmond. — Center Point Large Print edition.
pages cm
ISBN 978-1-61173-729-5 (Library binding : alk. paper)
1. Large type books. I. Title.
PS3535.I424W55 2013
813'.54—dc23

2012050625

To CARLTON F. WELLS

and the memory of
DONAL H. HAINES
(University of Michigan)

THE
WILD BREED

ONE

Curt Metheny stepped into the stirrup and swung his right leg across the worn leather. The tall steel-dust gelding stirred beneath him. Holding the horse in, Curt looked down at the two older men in the ranchyard, his face bitter and bleak.

Hooper Forbes hitched his belt over his sagging potbelly and said, "Sorry, boy, but that's how it is."

"It's all right," Curt Metheny said. "I wasn't expecting much."

"I know you're a good hand, Curt, though maybe you never worked too steady at it. But I ain't hiring now, not even top hands."

He don't want me around Lenora, Curt was thinking. *That's one reason.* But the other ranchers didn't have daughters like Lenora. There just wasn't a job for Curt Metheny on this range. He had suspected it before; now he knew for certain. This was the last stop, the one he had dreaded most. Nothing to do now but go back to town. And get drunk.

Doyle Guinness, the Frying Pan foreman, glanced up from the scuffed boot he was digging into the dirt. "Ever think of trying somewhere outside the Ontawee?"

Curt laughed shortly. "Time I did, I guess, Doyle."

"Good horse you got there," Guinness said

irrelevantly. "You ever want to sell, keep me in mind."

"I don't figure on selling."

Guinness scowled and spat tobacco juice. "You don't need a horse like that where you're working."

"That's for me to say," Curt said mildly. "Well, I'll see you—"

He kneed the big gray about and headed out of the yard. *The bastards,* he thought. *They won't give a man a chance. They get a man down and won't let him up.* But his time would come. Sooner or later he'd bust loose and show these highheaded augers something.

He felt heat rise in his lean cheeks and rim his ears with fire. He knew Forbes and Guinness were talking about him back there—about him and his family—and he could imagine what they were saying. It filled him with a fury that burned his throat and soured his stomach. He wanted to strike out at somebody, lash away with a gun or his bare hands at almost anyone. He'd have to cut loose before long.

A rider barreled around an outlying shed and came straight at Metheny, high and mighty like all the Frying Pan cowboys, expecting everyone to pull aside and make way for them. Curt held his mount on course, making the man on the smaller pony pull up short, swearing. It was Harry Keech, broad and squat in the saddle, with a grin on his battered face as his horse blocked the passage.

"What you doing way out here in cattle country, Curt?" he inquired with sly malice. "Reckon as how you didn't find Lenora home?"

"I wasn't looking for her."

Keech spat. "A sad case, a real pity. That gal still likes you, Curt; I know she does. A shame that old Hoop's dead set against you. Probably figures that jaybird Theron Ware's a better match, huh?"

"I don't know, Harry. And I don't care a damn." Metheny's voice was dull until he gave it a new edge: "You going to pull out, or you want me to ride right over that runty bronc?"

Keech's grin widened. "Always that chip on your shoulder, kid. Simmer down. Your horse *is* some bigger, but *you* ain't!"

"I'm big enough, Harry," said Curt Metheny, restraining himself with considerable effort.

Keech laughed and gestured. "Aw, we ain't got no call to fight, Curt. Put a check on that temper. You hear 'bout Utah Tyrrell's gang up in Arrowhead? Went in to take the Wells Fargo station and run into a trap. Got the hell shot outa them, from what I hear—cut plumb to pieces and choused outa town. First time Utah's bunch ever got set back real bad."

"Sorry to hear it," Curt said, annoyed at the man's relish of the news.

"You'd side them outlaws?"

"I favor the underdogs mostly."

Harry Keech barked with laughter. "I get it, Curt—being one yourself and all—Now don't get all het up, boy. I didn't mean nothing bad. There's worse things than shoveling horse dung outa livery barns."

"There is for a fact," agreed Metheny. "Like groveling in the same for the big moguls."

Keech stiffened and broadened in the leather. "Don't go prodding me too far, Curt. I never groveled, and I never will. And I ain't taking much more from you."

"You asked for it, Harry."

"All right, forget it," Keech mumbled, massaging his stubbled jowls. "You know, they say one of Utah Tyrrell's boys—maybe Utah himself—has got a girl in Holly. A gal named Rita that works in the Mustang Saloon."

"Is that so?" drawled Curt. "You got more news than the Holly Town *Herald*."

"Sure, I git around. And I like to study folks out. Now the boss's girl, that Lenora, is quite a gal under that fine smooth face she wears. I could tell you some things on her—"

"Drop it!" Curt Metheny said with wicked intensity. "That big mouth of yours, somebody's going to shut it for good someday."

Keech went solemn and ugly. "You, maybe?"

"Me—maybe." Curt watched the man's eyes, ready for anything.

"Aw, the hell with it and you too," Keech growled. "I got work to do."

Curt smiled. "I wouldn't want to keep you from that, Harry."

"You couldn't!" blustered Keech. "And don't think for a minute I'm scairt of you, boy—" Suddenly he was grinning again. "Was going to do you a favor, but I don't know. Going to tell you Lenora's out riding this afternoon, all by herself—or maybe to meet Theron Ware. But you ain't supposed to go near her, so you better keep away from that South Waterhole."

"I wouldn't think of trespassing."

"You're a smart boy—sometimes." Chortling, Keech yanked his pony aside and around the big gray. He called back over his shoulder: "Going to the dance come Saturday night?"

"I might."

"See you there. Come loaded and ready to turn loose your wolf."

Curt Metheny grimaced, shook his head, and let the gelding drift in the direction of the rutted wagon road that led to Holly Town. *I should have busted Keech,* he thought. But if you busted one Frying Pan rider, you had to take on the whole crew. Well, it would no doubt come to that, eventually.

He rode on at an easy, single-footed gait, glad to put this last ranch behind him, yet reluctant to return to town without a job. Back to Lauritsen's

13

livery stable, which had once belonged to Curt's father, and where he now worked as a hostler. Curt spat with distaste and raised his face to the wind from the open prairie. He could ride and rope and work stock with any of them, but his name was Metheny. That put the mark on him, branded him an outcast. The name Metheny was an evil legend in the Ontawee country.

He considered ranging round by the South Waterhole. It would be nice to see Lenora alone again. The thought stirred an old hunger deep inside him. There was an earthy streak in the girl, enough to make her fiery and fascinating. Traces of it showed in her eyes and about her mouth, in contrast to the fine cut of her features. Lenora must have got her looks from her mother's side. She had the look of a true thoroughbred, while old Hoop was as crude and gross as some of his low-down hired hands, a hog of a man, as greedy for money as he was for food.

Curt thought of the days when he and Lenny had planned to marry. They'd been very young then, and Curt had been accepted and welcome in the big house at Frying Pan. That was before the blight had fallen on the Metheny family.

Curt wondered why Keech had revealed the girl's whereabouts today. Perhaps he knew she was meeting Theron Ware and wanted Curt to tangle with the young banker. Or maybe Lyme Vector was working that part of the range, and

Keech figured Lyme might shoot Curt down for molesting the boss's daughter. But it didn't matter what Keech had at the back of his cunning mind. In his present mood, Curt Metheny wouldn't mind brawling with Ware or shooting it out with Vector. And he did want to see Lenora Forbes, regardless of the consequences.

She was the only girl he'd ever wanted with everything in him, all the way and forever. There'd been a few others that didn't really count—nights at the Mustang and other places.

He thought of Rita, who worked in the Mustang. He'd heard before that she had a man with Utah Tyrrell's band. Old Barnaby had spoken of it, but only as a rumor. Rita herself never talked about it, even to Curt, whom she had known most of her life. Curt had tried to pry some, too, being interested in making contact with an outfit like Tyrrell's, but Rita just smiled and clammed up tight. Curt had considered turning outlaw if he could make the right connections. A man who couldn't get a better job than hostler in the town livery barn might as well move outside the law. But it wasn't so simple, unless you wanted to set out on your own. It wasn't easy to hook up with a gang like Utah Tyrrell's. You had to have experience, a record, and a reputation—and Curt Metheny had nothing.

Curt swung the big gray away from the twin ruts of the wagon road toward the South

15

Waterhole. Perhaps there was a chance he'd catch Lenora up there alone. But if he had to shoot a man or two hereabouts, it might lead to a breakaway from Holly Town, and make him an eligible recruit for Utah Tyrrell's night riders. He loosened the Colt .44 in its holster and tried the Winchester in its sheath, almost hoping Lyme Vector or Theron Ware or somebody would come along looking for trouble.

TWO

If Lenora Forbes was in this valley, Curt knew where to find her. He stopped by the creek in the canyon below to water the big gray and drank deeply himself. Then he ducked his head, washed his face and hands, and wiped them dry with his blue bandanna. Contrary to custom, he wore his brown hair clipped short on his well-shaped skull. It was cleaner and cheaper, and in direct rebuttal to the long hair and sideburns affected by Theron Ware and other townsmen.

He crossed the grass toward a sentinel ridge with a lone ponderosa pine at its peak, which thrust up above the waterhole. Red cattle were scattered at graze on the parklike plain, where aspens made a silvery shimmer against the darkness of cedar, pine, and juniper. The cattle, fat and sleek with the Forbes Frying Pan brand burned high and large on the shoulder, looked up incuriously at the passing horseman and bent back to their grazing. The afternoon sun set the water agleam through the trees, and high against the molten blue an eagle soared in majestic flight. Swallows swooped in serene circles over the treetops, and the song of meadow larks floated on the breeze. Bright butterflies fluttered above purple-blooming lupine, and paintbrush made a vivid red stain alongside of a fallen cottonwood.

The air smelled sweet and pure, and Curt breathed it in with deep pleasure. A beautiful day in a beautiful land, and a girl like Lenora over yonder—

Her chestnut was alone, chomping grass in the shade of the ridge. Curt stepped down and let the split reins trail, and the big gray muzzled at once into the green forage. Curt walked toward the little glade near the water's edge, a trifle nervous and hesitant now but determined to keep going. The sight of Lenora sent a pleasant shock tingling through him. She sat with her back to that weathered gray log they had shared in the past, staring through quivering aspens at the sunlit sheen of water.

At the light crunch of his boots, Lenora rose and turned, and Curt wasn't certain whether her look showed just surprise, or surprise mixed with disappointment. There was no welcome in it, anyway, and they stood there, awkward and ill at ease, the intimate closeness of old completely gone from them. Lenora looked taller than she was, owing to her straight, supple bearing and high dark head. She wasn't beautiful, or even pretty, but she had something better, a look of distinction and quality. She was different, unique, and shaped with such loveliness, it made Curt catch his breath.

"Why, Curt," she murmured. "You—you really shouldn't be here."

"Why not?" The hurt turned him hard and rough.

"My father wouldn't like it. Theron wouldn't like it."

"The hell with them. But if you don't want me here, I'll go."

Lenora shook her head, hand lifted in a restraining motion. "It—it is quite a surprise, you know."

His smile was thin. "And not a happy one. You expecting Theron, Len?"

"I—I'm not sure."

"Well, sit down, Lenny," said Curt Metheny. "Can't do any harm to talk a few minutes now we got the chance. It's been a long time."

"Yes, Curt, it has."

She resumed her seat in the grass, back to the log, and Curt sat on the crumbling wood, not too near her.

"What you doing out of town, Curt?" she asked.

"Hunting a riding job."

"And you didn't find one?"

Curt's laugh was bitter. "You know I didn't. Not in this country."

Lenora turned brown grave eyes on his high-boned profile. "Why don't you go away somewhere, Curt? Where you'd have a chance to start again."

"I'm going, Len—if I ever get enough money to move out."

"You'd soon have enough if you didn't drink it all up."

His eyes were cold on her. "I see Theron's been doing some talking."

"Not only Theron. Everybody knows the life you're leading."

Head bent, he swore under his breath. "Why can't they leave me alone?"

"I don't know, Curt. But they can't—or won't." There was a sorrow in her that almost matched his, and it drew them closer together.

Curt stared straight at her. "What ever happened to us, Lenny?"

"It didn't happen to us, Curt." She smiled with that same sadness. "It wasn't us—it was outside. We had nothing to do with it."

His bronze features hardened. "I know—it was my folks. Are they going to hold that against me forever, Len?"

"I don't know. I'm afraid so, Curt. That seems to be the way people are."

"And you, too? You feel the same way, don't you?"

"No—No, I wouldn't, Curt—if you'd done different yourself. I fought my father, Theron, everybody, for quite a while. Then I got tired of fighting, I guess. *You* weren't fighting them, not the right way. You kept drinking and helling around, playing right into their hands."

"Maybe so, Len, but how can one man fight a whole town and range? Unless he takes to a gun. And then he don't last long."

"It does seem hopeless." Lenora sighed. "And perhaps it is—here. But you'd be all right somewhere else, Curt. You'd get along fine outside the Ontawee."

Metheny nodded dully. "Yeah, I got in a rut here, Len. Drifting along, sinking deeper all the time. Have to make a move—before it's too late." His sandy, cropped head lifted. "You going to marry Theron Ware?"

"Why, I don't know. He wants me to, and my folks are agreeable—"

"And you? You're the one that counts."

"I—I'm not sure. I like Theron. I don't know if it's love, but I enjoy being with him. He has a lot of charm."

"He's not good enough for you, Len," said Curt. "I'm not talking behind his back—I've told him that, and I'll tell him again."

"Theron's done very well in the bank," Lenora said. "J. A. Cottrell regards him highly, calls him his right-hand man. And he's liked and respected in Holly and all around the country."

Curt snorted softly and dug his bootheels. He knew about Theron Ware, who went to church regularly, sang in the choir, and then sneaked over to the Mustang. To Curt's mind he was a politician in the worst sense, a hand-shaking, back-slapping phony without a grain of decency, honesty, or sincerity in him. How could a character like that fool everybody?

"All right, Lenora," Curt drawled. "Theron's a success, and I'm a failure. But I wouldn't trade places with him. He can have everything else, Len, but I hope he never gets you."

The girl scanned Curt's taut profile. "You know something about Theron that other people don't? Something I should know."

"I've known him all my life, Len, and so have you. I used to like him, when we were kids. I don't any more—and it's not because he's up and I'm down. He's changed, that's all."

"He's ambitious, Curt. He wants to make something of himself."

"So he's ambitious. If you got to cut throats, stab backs, and stomp on faces to be ambitious, then I'm glad I'm not."

"You're bitter, Curt—"

Metheny laughed. "Haven't I got some right to be, Len?"

"Yes, I guess you have," Lenora murmured. "Now, tell me what I ought to know about Theron Ware."

He shook his head. "I won't tell you. Find out for yourself, Lenny. Ask the bartenders and store-keepers, the small ranchers and homesteaders, the town drunks and roustabouts."

"I can't believe that about Theron Ware," said Lenora. "He's always been a perfect gentleman with me."

"He's got some judgment and sense," Curt

admitted wryly. "And your father's big and rich enough to keep Theron in line—But I'm not asking you to believe anything, Lenny. I've talked too damn much already. It's not becoming to a man." He rose and stretched, and Lenora stood up beside him, her eyes darkly intent on his angular brown face. Curt smiled down at her. "I'll be riding along, Len."

The whisper of boots in grass and pine needles reached him then, even before the crisp voice cracked out the name *"Metheny!"* like an epithet. Curt drew and whirled in one swift motion, striding over the log and bringing his gun level and lined on the tall, white-shirted figure of Theron Ware. A cry of protest went up from Lenora, shrill and urgent, and Theron spread his hands.

"I'm not carrying a gun, Curt," he said.

There was no weapon in sight, so Curt, although he had suspected that Ware was never without a short belly-gun hidden somewhere, let the hammer down gently and slid the Colt back into the leather. "You could get yourself shot, Theron, coming up on a man that way."

"I'm not a gun fighter," Ware said, the words cold and clipped. "But I'll oblige you in any other way you want it. You have no business being here. You've been told to keep away. If you don't know your place, someone should teach you a lesson."

"You want to be the one, Theron?" drawled Metheny.

Walking in toward them, Ware was big and rangy, well-built, a handsome man in the white shirt, embroidered vest, dark pants, and shiny, ornamented boots. A white hat was raked back on his pomaded black hair, and curly sideburns framed his strong, ruddy features, the teeth flashing white beneath the neat mustache.

"I don't hold with fighting in front of a lady," Ware said with calm assurance. "But if you insist—"

"Tell the lady to take a walk," Curt suggested.

"I'm staying right here," Lenora Forbes declared. "There's nothing for you to fight about, anyway. Why don't you two boys grow up?"

Ware glanced at her. "Your father told you not to see any more of Metheny."

"I'm of age. I'll see whoever I please."

"Was this meeting prearranged, by any chance?"

Curt said, "Pure accidental. I just happened to ride by. Had an idea it was a free country. Maybe I was wrong?"

"You always seem to be wrong." Ware smiled with contempt. "For men like you this is not a free country—you don't belong in it. Now, get rid of that pistol."

"Stop this nonsense, you idiots!" Lenora said. "I ought to use this quirt of mine on both of you."

Curt unbuckled his belt and turned to place it on the log. "This won't take long, Len," he said, smiling at her.

Theron Ware lunged suddenly at Curt's back, hooked his right arm around his neck, setting his heels to wrench savagely upward and back. Locked helpless in that strangling grip, Curt was jerked over and down on top of the other man. Bucking and kicking violently, Curt tried to break the killing hold, but Ware's arm was a bar of iron under his chin, shutting off his breath and twisting his neck to a cruel angle. In vain Curt strove to butt his head back into Theron's face, before the increasing pressure could choke the life out of him. Finally, in desperation, Curt drove a vicious elbow deep into the banker's groin. With a gasping cry of agony Ware shuddered and lost his grip, and Curt rolled clear and free in the grass.

Neither was able to rise at once. When they did get up, slow and groggy, Curt was sobbing for breath and Ware was bent almost double. Curt's neck felt broken. For a banker, Theron was mighty powerful. Curt had nearly lost this one in the first minute. A little longer, and he'd have been out cold, maybe dead. Lenora watched them with wide eyes and parted lips, wringing the braided quirt in her white-knuckled hands.

Curt's lungs were just beginning to function when Ware straightened up and came forward in a snarling rush. Curt was slow in raising his weighted arms, and Theron's fists smashed into his face, rocking his head and setting off flares behind his eyeballs. Curt gave ground and grappled at the flailing arms, finally getting a hold to fling Ware aside and slip clear himself.

As Theron came about again, Curt was in on him, hooking a left to the mouth, ripping a right into the belly. Ware grunted and broke in the middle once more, but he kept on swinging, and Curt couldn't get a clean shot at him. Dust smoked up as they circled and weaved, both bleeding and panting hard now, lunging and striking until they got tangled up and went reeling crazily back and forth, with Ware constantly trying to get a crippling knee into Metheny's crotch.

Curt crouched and sledged wickedly at Theron's body, left and right, getting his shoulders and back and legs into the blows. Ware staggered back, and Curt switched to the face, lashing Ware's head from one side to the other, the pomaded hair splintering into wild shards of glossy black. "You fight—so fair—banker," Curt gasped out, and went after the man with brute fury. Catching the back of the bowed neck, Curt yanked Ware's head downward and lifted his right knee into the face with terrible force. The sodden smash was sickening, even to Curt, and Ware went slack and limp, dropping instantly with his ruined face buried in a bed of ferns.

"Curt—you've killed him!" Lenora said in hushed horror.

"No—but I ought to." Curt stood swaying on shaky legs, blood and sweat streaming from his face, chest and shoulders heaving in painful convulsions. "Have to—sooner or later. If he don't—kill me first."

Minutes later, Theron Ware was beginning to stir and roll feebly about on the ground, and Curt was reaching down to help him up when a crashing in the brush brought him erect and spinning round—too late. A rider had burst into the clearing, and his rope was already snaking out with a blurred *swish*. Curt tried to dodge, but the loop settled and tightened about his arms and body, biting to the bone. It was Lyme Vector on his favorite sorrel, Curt saw in the fleeting instant before he was hauled off his feet and dashed against the earth.

Vector wheeled the sorrel and used his spurs, putting the horse into a run that kept the rope taut and dragged Metheny along the rough ground like a broken ragdoll, bouncing and twisting grotesquely in a torrent of dust. Lenora's scream came from far away: "Stop, Lyme! Pull up, you fool!" Then the brush was clawing and slashing at Curt Metheny, and he was barely conscious when Theron Ware's great shout reached Vector and caused him to rein up at last.

"Hold it, Lyme!" yelled Ware, mouth distended

in the crimsoned mask of his face. "Bring him back here, man. He's got something coming from me!"

Lyme Vector turned back and heaved on the lariat, jerking Curt upright and holding him there, the rope binding and cutting into his arms. "You're plain lucky I didn't drag you to death," Vector gritted with icy venom, towering in the saddle, buck teeth bared in his beaked face. "But maybe Theron's got a better treatment for you. Come on, move along now. Walk, boy, or I'll drag you back in on your face!"

Stumbling weak-kneed along beside the sorrel, Curt strained to loosen the numbing loop, but Lyme was keeping his rope tight as a bowstring. Lyme would have dragged him to death all right, if they hadn't stopped it, and now Theron would probably beat him to death—or shoot him to ribbons. With a cold fear spreading in his stunned brain, Curt knew he was helpless in the hands of two men who hated his guts, who had hated him for years. The father of Theron Ware and the father of Lyme Vector had been members of the posse that went out into the Potholes after Jud Metheny years ago, and they had been two of the men who died there under Jud Metheny's guns. Nothing was apt to stop Theron and Lyme now that they had their chance at Curt.

"What are you going to do, Theron?" demanded Lenora Forbes as Vector halted his sorrel and yanked Curt erect before them. "Haven't you done enough to him? He's half-dead now."

"That's not half enough," Theron Ware said, spitting out a mouthful of blood.

"Want him turned loose, Theron?" Lyme asked.

"Not yet. Hold him up there, Lyme."

Ware stepped forward and chopped brutally at Curt Metheny's blackened face, and Curt would have gone down if it hadn't been for the taut rope. Ware set himself to strike again, his split lips skinned back on reddened teeth, when Lenora Forbes lifted Curt's gun from the log and spoke with sharp authority:

"*That's enough, Theron!* I've got a gun on you, and you know I can use it. Don't touch Curt again, or I will. Turn him loose, Lyme, *right now!* And then keep away from him, both of you."

Theron Ware glanced back in astonishment and saw the big .44 firm and steady in Lenora's grasp. Lyme Vector swung off the sorrel, and Curt collapsed the moment the rope slackened. Lyme loosened and freed his loop and stepped back, a questioning look at Ware.

Theron shook his battered head. "She's right, Lyme. This has gone far enough. Get some water for him." The cold light in Lenora's eyes had chilled Theron Ware back to sanity.

Vector's beaver teeth showed still more over the rope he was coiling with tender care. "I ain't taking orders from you, Theron; git your own water." He mounted the sorrel, a lank figure with great shoulders and arms. "You shoulda let me finish him. Someday you'll wish you had, mister. You want me any more, Miss Lenora?"

"No, I don't want either of you," the girl said, still holding the Colt level in her tanned hand. "I'll take care of Curt. You go too, Theron."

"What's come over you, Lenora?" asked Theron Ware, with a gesture of dismay. "Are you out of your mind? I won't leave you with *him*."

Lyme Vector was already riding away, and Lenora Forbes lined the .44 fully on Ware, the hammer back under her thumb joint.

"Yes, you'll leave me right here—with him," she said with icy clearness. "I wouldn't mind shooting you, Theron. After seeing what you just did."

Ware gazed at her in bewilderment. "He smashed my face, didn't he? My nose is broken. What do you—"

"Get out, Theron," said Lenora. "I'm sick of the sight of you."

Theron Ware walked slowly away. "I'll kill him next time," he said, teeth grating on edge. "Or let Lyme kill him."

Lenora was already kneeling beside Curt Metheny, but when Ware glanced back at her, she lifted the gun in his direction and held it there until he disappeared in the brush and timber.

When Curt surfaced to light and reality, he was

surprised to find himself still alive, and even more surprised to find Lenora Forbes at his side. Lyme Vector and Theron Ware had intended to kill him. Curt knew it, even before those last punches had knocked him senseless and sagging in the tight rope. Len must have stopped them. He saw his gun in the grass beside her then and knew she had saved his life. He stared up at her with dim awe and wonder.

Lenora had bathed his head and face, washed the blood and dirt from his shoulders, arms, chest, and back. His tattered shirt was spread to dry on the ground nearby.

"You took a beating, Curt, lost some skin and blood," said the girl. "But I couldn't find any broken bones."

"I'm all right, Lenny—thanks to you," he said, slow and wondering. "You must've turned my gun on them."

"I had to, Curt. They were going to kill you—or cripple you for life. I never saw that side of Theron before."

"My dad killed both of their fathers, out in the Potholes that time."

"Then it—it won't end here, Curt?"

"It's only just begun, Len."

"Oh, Curt, I don't know—" She sighed and bent forward and lowered her mouth upon his, still murmuring: "But it won't work—for us. It never can be—not for us, not here—"

31

His bare arms closed round her, and the pressure of his mouth stilled her lips, crushed and held them full and sweet and opening in warm response. Time ceased as he turned on his side and drew her even closer, her body firmly soft and vibrant against his.

"You feel so good, Curt—" she breathed huskily, her arms clinging and straining.

"It's still there for us," he said. "It always will be."

"No, Curt." Lenora fought to break away with abrupt violence, and after an agonizing minute he let her go. She sat upright in the grass, her full bosom rising and falling, a tortured look on her fine face. "I've got to get home—before dark. And you've got a long ride into town."

The magic was gone. Curt got up, dazed and stiff, feverish and lightheaded, and lifted the girl to her feet. She moved away at once. Curt pulled on the damp, torn shirt, shrugged into the leather vest, and strapped on his gunbelt. She had sent his blood racing, and the beat of his heart left him breathless.

With eyes averted, Lenora handed him his hat. "How do you feel?"

"Not too bad—considering."

In a kind of trance, they walked out toward their horses, well apart and almost like strangers again, the breech widening between them at every step. Curt spoke at last, forcing the slow words out:

"I guess it's no use, Len—not for us."

"I—I'm promised to Theron," she said, her voice shaky and strained. "There's too much—too many things against us, Curt. You're good—and decent. You're a fine boy, Curt. I'm sorry about—everything."

THREE

The moon had risen when Curt Metheny reined up on the ridge above the ghost town of Lodestone, and its light laid a jigsaw pattern of black and silver upon the broken landscape. The old mining camp straggled along the gulch of Kenoshee Creek. It was said to be haunted, but Curt figured that Spider Werle, the sole remaining resident, had spread such rumors to keep people away. Most travelers bypassed the place, especially at night, but Curt generally rode straight through the deserted settlement and often stopped to listen to the fantastic yarns of Spider Werle. The aged hermit still believed he would strike it rich here, start another gold rush, and bring Lodestone back to booming life. "They'll all come back when I make my hit," he declared, "including the dead along with the living."

The town was eerie and unreal in the moonlight, as Curt Metheny rode in, the hushed stillness broken only by the rustling of the wind. The ruined buildings seemed to be sinking into the desolate earth, with dirt and debris drifted high against the walls, overflowing porches and thresholds. There were caved-in soddies, skeletal shacks and sheds, crumbling adobes, and disjointed frame structures with gaping windows, sagging overhangs, and doors and shutters twisted askew. Moonbeams glistened on faded signs, some of which were still faintly legible, and Curt had heard legends linked with those names. His father and old Barnaby had known these places in their youth, lived and loved, drunk and gambled, fought and killed here. Barney didn't talk much about it, but Curt had heard the stories from other sources.

After the clean grass and sage of the open plains, this gulch smelled of decay and death. He caught a glimpse of bats flapping erratically through the shadows. The sound of rats scurrying and scratching in the rubble came to him, and then above it the stomp of hoofs and the snort of a horse somewhere ahead. There was another rider in Lodestone tonight, and Curt reined his big gray to a standstill. Theron Ware or Lyme Vector—or both of them—might be staked out here to bushwhack him. And he'd heard it rumored that Rita Corday sometimes came here to meet her lover from Utah Tyrrell's band.

Curt pulled into an alley, stepped down, and ground-tied the gray, then moved forward on foot, the .44 Colt in his right hand. The sounds had come from the area of the town corral, and now the murmur of talking reached his ears. A man and woman—it sounded like Rita, and she was not alone this night. If the man was one of the Tyrrell gang, perhaps Curt could join up with them. Rita would vouch for him, even though she didn't want him to turn outlaw. But when the man spoke again, Curt recognized the voice and knew it was no bandit. It was Stan Russett, a deputy marshal from Holly Town.

Curt paused to listen at the building corner, beneath the drooping boards of a shattered awning. The jumble of old corrals lay beyond, with broken bars and poles canted like jackstraws in the moonlight. Rita was leaning against the outer rails of the first pen, and Stan Russett was standing in front of her, tall and straight and full of his own dignity and importance. A smug and stupid man, Stan had grown into since he and Curt had been boys together, and it saddened and angered Curt to see the change in him.

"I still don't see why you should follow me out here," Rita was saying.

"In the line of duty," Stan Russett said. "I thought you might be meeting one of Tyrrell's boys—or Utah himself."

"You want to be a hero, don't you, Stan?"

"No, ma'am," Stan Russett said. "I'm just a lawman trying to do the job as best he can."

Rita's laugh, light and musical, held a hint of mockery. "Now that you know I don't have a rendezvous with an outlaw, you can ride back to town."

"Thought I heard a rider coming in, Rita."

"If you did, it was no one looking for me."

"I'll escort you home."

"You're very gallant," Rita Corday said, "but I'm not ready to go—yet."

Stan Russett's laughter was humorless. "Well, the night's young and you're real pretty under the moon. You know I've always liked you, Rita."

"I'm flattered, Stan. But I can't return the compliment."

"I know." He kicked dirt against the lower rails. "It was always Jack Metheny. You couldn't see anybody else. Well, you got what you deserved when he deserted you. And he got what he had coming—from the Sioux."

Rita smiled sadly. "Don't speak unkindly of the dead. And please go, I want to be alone."

"No, by God! You can't order me round like a dog. You try to act like a great lady, when you're nothing but—"

"Not quite," Rita said calmly. "I have the privilege of refusing anyone I don't want. You and Theron Ware should know that—by this time."

Stan Russett caught her by the shoulders and jerked her roughly off the bars. "I'm not good enough for a little tramp like you. I'll show you!" He wrenched her in close and bent to search for her mouth. Rita turned her head away, stamped a high heel down on his instep, and lifted a sharp knee against him. Grunting and cursing in pain, Stan let go of her and stumbled backward. As he lurched forward again, Rita raised her quirt.

"Don't come near me, mister. I'll slash your face wide open!"

They stood frozen in that tense moonlit tableau, and Curt Metheny, his gun back in its sheath, stepped out from under the wrecked overhang. "I don't think the lady cares for your company, Stan," he drawled.

Stan Russett swiveled to face him, bug-eyed with surprise, and went into a gunman's crouch.

"Go ahead, Stan—reach for it," said Curt, arms hanging loose at his sides.

Russett couldn't bring himself to the point of drawing. With a long, ragged sigh he dropped his hands and scowled at Metheny. "What the hell you prowling round out here for, anyway?"

"Just riding through," Curt said. "I ought to shoot you for molesting Rita. Or beat what few brains you got out of that rock-head of yours."

Rita Corday said, "Don't waste a bullet on him, Curt. Just send him on his way."

"So, it's that way with you two?" sneered Stan Russett. "Little brother Curt crawling into big brother Jack's love nest, huh? Ain't that romantic?"

"Shut your filthy mouth!" Curt Metheny said. "Or I'll put one right through that tin star you're so proud of."

"Maybe you want to shed that gun and try it barehanded?"

"Any way you call it. You never saw the day you could lick a Metheny."

"Maybe I couldn't lick Jack. But you ain't as big as your brother was."

"I'm a lot meaner though," Curt said, with a grin. "Try me and see, Stanko."

Russett winced at the nickname Jack Metheny had tagged him with in boyhood days. "Hell, I got more important things to do than beat up bums and stableboys. But I'm going to get you one of these days, Curt, and get you good."

"Shut up and blow," Curt said. "The only beatings you ever handed out were to dead-drunk cowboys, and then you used a gun barrel—from behind. Get out of here, Stanko."

Russett turned away with an angry gesture, mounted his black horse, jabbed hard with his spurs, and rode out at a gallop toward Holly Town.

"Glad you came along, Curt—just then," Rita murmured, smiling up at him.

"You could have handled him yourself, Rita, but it was a pleasure for me to move in." Curt threw a friendly arm around her shoulders. "I should've smashed him, though."

"No, he isn't worth it. I don't mind his insults— I know what's behind them." Rita shook her head, the coppery hair burnished by moonbeams. "You've got enough troubles in Holly, without taking Stan on—Did you have a fight today, Curt?"

He nodded, with a rueful grin, and told her what had happened on the Frying Pan range. Rita listened with interest and sympathy, a tragic beauty in her clean, sculptured face and sorrowful slanted eyes.

"Oh, Curt, I wish you could get away from here," she said. "I'd miss you terribly, but you'd be so much better off somewhere else."

"You could help me, Rita. If you really know one of Utah Tyrrell's men."

"I won't have you turning outlaw, Curt. That's no way to live, either."

"It's better than this. At least, I'd feel like a man."

"A hunted man, an outcast."

"I'm an outcast right here, Rita. In my own home town."

"But you're within the law, Curt. You're not a criminal, a fugitive, a wanted man with a price on your head."

"You do know one of them, Rita?"

She inclined her head. "I've met all of them. They've been at the Mustang."

"Isn't there one in particular?"

"No, there couldn't be—not really. Not after Jack. He was my man. There'll never be anyone else for me."

Curt studied her sad, lovely profile. "Didn't you expect to meet one of them out here tonight?"

"No, Curt. I just like to come here, to get away by myself. My mother used to sing in that old opera house over there."

"Yes, I know," Curt murmured. "They say she was very beautiful. What are those night riders like, Rita?"

"Just men—like most other men. Except they have to be harder, tougher, and wilder, and they get that look—the haunted look of wild animals, hounded and hunted and fighting for their lives. You want to be like that, Curt?"

"Am I any better off this way?" Curt rolled two cigarettes and flicked a sulphur match alight on his thumbnail. "The whole Ontawee's against me, you know that, Rita." He lit her smoke, then his own. "At least those men have got one another. And I've got nobody—I'm all alone."

Rita Corday smiled fondly up at him. "You don't mean that, Curt. You've got Dane Lauritsen and little Tee Dee and old Barnaby. You've got Lenora Forbes—and me."

"Yes, you're partly right." Curt touched her shining hair. "I can count on you, Rita—and Barney and Tee Dee. But Dane is souring on me—and I sure haven't got Lenora."

"Well, with three of us, you aren't exactly alone, Curt."

"I appreciate that, Rita. I'm thankful for you three—What kind of a man is Utah Tyrrell, would you say?"

Rita puffed thoughtfully on her cigarette. "A good man gone wrong. Tall and strong, steady and sound, quiet and easy. A handsome man, almost noble looking—except for an ugly birthmark on one side of his face."

"And the others, Rita?"

"A Mexican called Spanish, a half-breed Indian called Comanche, an old-timer named Pitts. Two boys, Kid Ansted and Dusty Shands, even younger than you, Curt. Two real bad ones, natural born killers, Bowie Bowden and Herm Goedert. And a one-eyed man they call Jakes, strange and silent, set off from the rest, sad and lonesome. More like Utah than the others, yet all by himself—alone."

"I'd like to know them," Curt Metheny said, boyish and wistful. "I'd like to ride with them, Rita. I'd feel alive then, I think."

"But not for long, Curt," said Rita. "You'd soon be dead—just like they will be."

"Did you hear anything about them up in Arrowhead?"

"There are stories going around. I don't know how true they are. But if they didn't get it there, they'll get it some other place. It's bound to happen. You can't buck those long odds forever."

The despair in her voice and her face led Curt to change the subject, thinking that she cared more for somebody in the Tyrrell outfit than she wanted to confess.

They left the ghost town several minutes later and took the trail toward Holly across open rolling prairie. Curt tried as usual to disregard the dark smudge of decrepit structures that marked the old Parkhurst layout, but his glance strayed in that direction in spite of himself. A familiar chill of horror set him to shivering in the leather, and the nausea in his stomach made him gag. Rita Corday looked at him with quick warm sympathy, but there was nothing to say.

In that ranch house, a log-faced dugout built into the hillside, Curt's mother and Zed Parkhurst had died—violent deaths in gunsmoke. And from that spread Judson Metheny, Curt's father, had started his last lone flight, down through the Sand Hills and out into the Pothole country, where death had caught up with him, too.

A few miles farther on, Rita Corday spoke: "I hear that young Alvah Parkhurst is gunning for you too, Curt."

Metheny grinned bleakly. "A big bag of wind. He's been threatening for a long time, they tell me. But I've never laid eyes on him, that I know of, Rita."

"Oh, Curt, I wish you'd get out of here before something happens—something bad. I wish both of us could get away. The Ontawee never brought us anything but heartbreak and sorrow."

"We'll make it someday, Rita," said Curt. "But I want to leave my mark on Holly Town before I go. I've got a lot of scores to settle here."

"Don't turn killer, Curt," pleaded Rita. "Something inside a man dies when he turns killer."

"I feel dead inside now," he said simply. "Maybe that'll give me an advantage, when the showdown comes—"

FOUR

Curt finished forking hay into the feed racks and walked back toward the lantern-lit arch of the livery stable. It had been a long day in the stables, and he couldn't take many more of them. It was no kind of work for a man like him. He hoped Tee Dee had the water heated and ready for his bath. Twenty-four hours after the fight at the waterhole, Curt Metheny was still lame and sore. Nobody had come after him yet, although he'd been on the lookout for Frying Pan riders all day. Evidently Theron Ware was keeping out of sight until his face healed up.

Curt had to get out of this town, but first he'd have to raise some money. There were people he could always borrow drinking money from—old Barnaby and Rita Corday and Tee Dee—but borrowing enough for a stake was a different proposition. Lauritsen was a possibility, but not a very strong one. Dane didn't approve of Curt's conduct of late, and didn't want to let him go, anyway. Curt was a good hand with horses, a hard worker all around, and Dane Lauritsen still hoped to reform him otherwise.

The great barn smelled of hay and grain, dust and manure, oiled leather and horses. As a boy Curt had loved those smells, but now he hated them. The odor of the stable seemed to cling to him, even after bathing and changing clothes, a stigma, a perpetual reminder of his low station in life. This had been a wonderful playground when his father owned it, and all the kids in town had hung around there with Jack and Curt, frolicking in the hayloft, playing hide-and-seek in stalls and sheds, romping about the corrals and feed pens, watching the bronc peelers tame the wild ones in the breaking corral.

Those had been happy times, even if the boys hadn't fully realized it then. Jud Metheny had been about the most popular man in Holly, outranking the younger element. Jack and Curt and their friends—Theron Ware, Stan Russett, Lyme Vector, and the rest—haunted the stable and yards. Here they had learned to harness, saddle, and tend to horses, driven their first rigs and ridden their first ponies. Jud had been generous—too generous for his own good. All the kids had worshiped him, and Jack and Curt had been looked up to because their father was Jud Metheny, who could ride anything on four legs, handle a gun and a rope like a magician, lick any man who crossed him, and make the best saddles in the West. *But that was a long way back,* Curt mused, *in another and far better world.*

Dane Lauritsen, busy over his books at the old roll-top desk in the glassed-in office, looked up and beckoned as Curt turned away from racking the pitchfork. Curt entered the office with some reluctance. He liked this gaunt spare man, but he did not want any lecture tonight.

"So you didn't land a riding job yesterday, Curt?" asked Lauritsen, his balding head tilted and the yellow-gray mustache drooping on his mournful face.

"They weren't hiring. Not me, anyway."

"You got into some more trouble though," Lauritsen said with characteristic bluntness. "Trouble at Frying Pan."

"Not of my making, Dane," said Curt, wondering anew at the way news traveled around this vast, lonely land.

"But you'll get blamed, of course."

"That figures. I always do."

"You've got the name of being a trouble-maker," Dane Lauritsen said gravely. "Whether you deserve it all or not, I cannot say, but the reputation sticks and follows a man. I had hoped you'd straighten out and settle down before now, Curt."

"There are times you have to fight, Dane. When it's forced on you, what else can you do?"

"I know, Curt. A man can't back down and run away. But you're always too ready. Maybe you don't exactly look for it, but you're always ready to fight. You can't lick this whole town and country all by yourself, Curt. Men who try to do that end up outlaws."

"They won't let me alone, Dane. They're always on me."

"I don't know, Curt. I think half the slurs and insults you jump at are in your own imagination. You're apt to think folks are running you down, talking about you—and your family—when they aren't at all. I been thinking of giving you an interest in this business, Curt, with a chance of working up to a full partnership. It's no more than you deserve, no more than I owe you—and your family. But you go on drinking and fighting—and hating all mankind. I can't do it, Curt, unless you change. Won't you at least make an effort, son?"

"Yeah, I'll try to, Dane," said Curt dully.

"Fine, Curt, fine—if you really mean it." Dane Lauritsen's solemn features lighted hopefully. "You stay sober and out of trouble, save some of your wages and act decent and respectable, and I'll see you get your chance."

"I'm obliged to you, Dane," said Curt, with shy, boyish awkwardness. "You been good and square to me, and I appreciate it."

"My uncle Eric brought all that misery onto your family, Curt," said Lauritsen somberly. "It all commenced with him. I came here to try and make it up to them, but I was too late—for your folks, anyway. Least I can do, I figure, is help you out a little, son."

"You couldn't help what Eric did, Dane. It wasn't your fault, in any way."

"I want to make up for it—I got to make up for it as much as I can, Curt. Go ahead and get washed up now."

Curt left the office and limped wearily toward his quarters at the rear of the stable. He would have liked to please Lauritsen, but Dane's way was too dull, too slow for him. Curt wanted to blow Holly Town hell-west-and-crooked all over the Ontawee plains.

Tee Dee had a pint of whiskey waiting for him, and the water steaming slightly in the huge round cask. Curt took a couple of swigs, passed the bottle to Tee Dee, and stripped off his work clothes. The barren room looked friendly, almost homelike, in the mellow lamplight. Curt tested the water, climbed into the barrel, and settled down with a long sigh of pleasure, only his head above the surface, a cigar in his teeth. Watching him worshipfully, little Tee Dee laughed in sheer delight.

"You sure look funny in the tub with that cigar! You feeling any better now, Curt?"

"A lot better since I got in here, Tee Dee. Guess maybe I'll live, after all."

"Wish you'd tell me about yesterday," Tee Dee said, sipping the whiskey like sarsparilla. He was a small, thin youngster with a withered left arm, a crooked back, and the face of an angel under kinky black curls.

"Hey boy, easy on that liquor," Curt warned

him, laughing through cigar smoke. "I told you what happened, Tee Dee."

"You ain't worth a damn as a storyteller, Curt. Did Dane call you down any?"

"Not much, kid. Just about what I deserved, probably."

"He's a good man, Dane is," the boy said. "Some different than Eric Lauritsen, from all I hear. You ever feel like going after Eric with a gun for what he done to your dad?"

"Yeah, I have, Tee Dee. But that's long past, and nobody knows where Eric went to. Even Dane don't know."

Tee Dee leaned back on the bunk, rubbing his hump against the wall. "You think Utah Tyrrell's bunch'll ever hit this way, Curt?"

"Hard to tell, Tee Dee," said Curt. "But I wish they would."

"Sure like to see 'em," Tee Dee murmured. "But they got shot up pretty bad in Arrowhead, according to what everybody's saying. Most likely have to lay low awhile, huh? The whole country out after 'em. Boy, that must be the life!"

"At least you live—until you die."

"Don't everybody?"

"No, Tee Dee," said Curt Metheny. "A lot of people just go through the motions."

"Yeah, I get what you mean. You like to join up with Utah Tyrrell, Curt?"

"I've thought of it some. But there isn't much chance—for me."

"Why not?" demanded Tee Dee. "You'd make 'em a good man, Curt. You're as tough as any of 'em, and just as good with guns and horses. Better'n most of 'em, I bet."

Curt Metheny laughed softly. "Bring me a drink, Tee Dee. And take away this cigar."

When the boy had gone out to supper, Curt stood up and soaped himself with thorough care before sinking back into the warm, luxurious depths. As he soaked there, drowsily at ease, his mind went back to the younger happier days, when the name of Metheny had been an honored and respected one.

Judson Metheny had built up the livery business in Holly, with funds acquired one way and another from Lodestone, and had prospered at it—until he took Eric Lauritsen in as a partner. Leaving the stable largely to Eric thereafter, Jud had resumed his saddle- and harness-making, concentrating on the craft he loved and had mastered.

Absorbed and lost in this work, Jud paid less and less attention to the business and financial affairs of the livery barn, although Barnaby tried to warn him that Eric was letting the place go to pot and ruin, and no doubt stealing Jud blind besides. But Jud trusted Eric Lauritsen, and it came as a complete and crushing shock to him, when Eric took off one day with all the company money, leaving nothing behind but a stack of bills that Jud had assumed were long since paid. Jud Metheny was never the same man after that.

He had to mortgage the business to pay off the debts, and it left him flat broke. When the bank foreclosed on the livery stable, Jud could have done well enough making saddles and harnesses, but by that time he was drinking heavily. It got so bad he couldn't carry on his trade, and the saddle shop went under, too. Domestic problems complicated matters and drove Jud to total distraction—and even harder drinking.

Jud hadn't used a gun much since the old days, when Lodestone was on the boom, but now he turned against humanity and took to the gun once more. Barnaby kept him out of a dozen shooting scrapes, and Ed Gracey averted gunplay in other instances, but it was bound to happen sooner or later. One day Jud wounded two men in a gun fight outside the Ten-High Saloon, and when the brother of one of the victims came after him later, Jud shot and killed the man. It was self-defense—the dead man had been a professional gun sharp—but Jud Metheny was getting meaner all the time, and public opinion ran high against him.

From there on the family deteriorated rapidly. Jud and his wife Martha had always got along fine, but under the pressure of poverty they began to quarrel constantly. What had been a happy home became a screaming madhouse, a place of horror. Jack, the older boy, took up drinking, gambling, and carousing in full scale with his girl Rita Corday. Amanda, the daughter, grew wild, unruly and man-crazy. Curt, the youngest of the family, still shuddered at the memory of those hideous days and nights, with the home and the world he loved going to pieces all around him.

When Jud and Martha weren't tearing one another apart, they were berating and scolding Jack and Amanda; and when Jack and Amanda were not under the lashing tongues of their parents, they were reviling one another. Curt wanted to run away from home, but he was afraid, and he didn't know where he'd go or what he'd do after he got there.

Jack was the first to break away from the degeneration of the Metheny family. He enlisted in the Seventh Cavalry, in time to go north with Custer on that spring campaign in 1876, and to die at the Little Big Horn. Ten years ago now. Curt had been fifteen at the time, too young for Jack to take along with him.

Rita Corday, the girl Jack had left behind, went to work in the Mustang to make her living. Then Amanda disappeared with a flashy young faro dealer from the Silver Queen, and the last heard of her, she was seen in a Kansas City saloon.

The inevitable climax had been even more of a

nightmare, with Judson Metheny coming home crazy-drunk and thrashing Martha, blaming her for the loss of Amanda and Jack—But Curt refused to think any more about the ultimate breakdown. He had tormented himself enough for one evening. He rose, rinsed himself, and climbed out of the barrel.

He had dressed and was pouring himself a drink when he heard someone shuffling along the stable floor. He looked around to see old Barnaby in the doorway.

"Come in, Barney, and have a drink," Curt said, glad as ever to see the old man, who had been his father's life-long friend. Barnaby was now janitor at the bank and handyman at the Mustang.

"Right cosy here, Curt. How are you, my boy?" Barnaby stumped in, a bent, gnarled, gray oak of a man, quite deaf now, his faded, sunken eyes alert, watching Curt's lips to read the answer.

"Not too bad, Barney." Curt poured another whiskey and handed it to the old-timer.

"Guess Theron and Lyme didn't use you up too awful bad. Theron didn't show in the bank today. I hear he ain't near as pretty as he was, son."

"Anybody miss him?"

"Nobody but old J. A. and a few bird-brained female customers." Barnaby sank into the raw-hide chair to nurse his drink, and Curt sat on the edge of the bunk. "Too bad, Curt, you didn't burn down both of them bastards yesterday."

"Then I'd really have to haul out of here, Barney."

"Still thinking of pulling out, Curt? And still needing a stake, I reckon. Well, I might have something for you, if you want to run the risk of it."

"I'm about ready to try most anything," Curt confessed.

"I got it fairly straight, son, that Rita's going to have a special visitor someday soon. Right from Utah Tyrrell's wild bunch. There's a reward on all them boys, Curt, and it would give you stake enough to travel on—if you're set on going. Hate to hurt Rita, or turn in a good outlaw, but somebody's bound to get him sometime. Rather it be you than some stinking lawdog like Stan Russett."

"Well, I don't know, Barney," said Curt. "Rita told me she had no special man with Utah, but I figured she was covering up. I like Rita a whole lot, and she's suffered enough from one Metheny. And my sympathy inclines toward the Tyrrell gang—if anywhere. But it's worth thinking over, Barney, and I'm obliged."

"It ain't an idea I'm too proud of myself," Barnaby admitted, grinning. "But if a man needs money bad enough—well, it's better'n robbing a bank. From a legal viewpoint, at least."

Curt joined in Barney's ironic laughter, and said, "Another thing, too. If I can reform enough, Dane says he'll take me into the business here."

"That is something to consider real serious, son. Dane's a solid man, and you'd make a good team. But reforming's a mighty painful task, they tell me. Never felt called on to try it myself."

Curt smiled over the cigar he was relighting. "If I'm ever saved, Barney, it won't be in this town. The way they got me tagged here, sprouting a pair of wings wouldn't do me any good."

"A damn shame, too," Barnaby grumbled, sucking whiskey from his gray mustache. "You was never a bad one, Curt. And don't let 'em turn you bad, neither. Or make you think your folks was bad."

"But that's in the books, Barney. You can't argue that off."

"I would, Curt. It was circumstances, fate, something—I'll never begin to know or understand what. But I *knew* your dad and ma. They was good people, the best. Good people can go wrong if life kicks 'em in the teeth enough times."

"Sure, I know, Barney," said Curt hollowly. "They were fine—then something happened to them. Let's go get some supper."

Emerging from the livery runway into Front Street, they met Stan Russett, an arrogant sternness on his hawklike features. Ignoring Barnaby, Stan paused with thumbs in gunbelt and surveyed Curt with cold insolence. Curt stared straight back, striving to contain and control his sudden anger.

"You want something of me, Stan?" he inquired finally.

"If I did, I'd take it." Russett spat and strode away, tall and stiff with self-importance.

Barnaby sent a vicious spurt of tobacco juice after the deputy. "That tin star makes Stan ten feet tall—he thinks. I can remember when he wouldn't of had any grub to eat or clothes to wear if it hadn't been for you Methenys."

"Stanko remembers it too, Barney," said Curt quietly. "Maybe that's one reason he hates me now. It sure is funny how growing up changes folks."

"It spoils the hell outa most of 'em, that's a fact," Barnaby agreed glumly.

As they moved on toward the eating houses, they encountered men who spoke to Barnaby but failed to see Curt Metheny at his side. Ed Gracey, the town marshal, stepped out from a deep-shadowed overhang and greeted them both with easy friendliness: "Evening, Barney. Hullo, Curt—I hope you aren't looking for anybody."

"Just for some supper, Ed," said Curt. "Any Frying Pan in town?"

"A few of the boys. Didn't see Lyme Vector or Harry Keech, though." Ed Gracey was a solid, stubby man with kind eyes and a low voice. Well along in years, he still moved with catlike ease and precision.

"I won't look for them, Ed," said Curt Metheny. "But they're apt to come hunting for me."

"Not while I'm around, Curt," murmured Ed Gracey, and he dropped back into the shadows beneath the board awning.

"They'll come just the same," Barnaby growled as they trod onward over the splintered plank walk. "Ed can't be everywhere at once."

"Sure, they'll come—Hooper Forbes'll send them," Curt said. "And Theron will try something. Or hire somebody to do it for him."

"Yeah, they'll all be in Saturday night for the shindig," Barnaby predicted gloomily. "You better stay sober that night, son—if you're still in town."

Curt nodded absently. He was thinking about the night rider who was coming in to see Rita Corday. He didn't really want to take a man like that, even for the reward money. Ever since that posse had run down his father, an army against one lone man in the Potholes, Curt's sympathies had been with the hunted. But maybe he could persuade the outlaw to take him along to meet Utah Tyrrell and perhaps join up with them.

Curt had two widely divergent dreams. In one he was married to Lenora Forbes, with a home and a small spread of his own, and kids to raise as time went on. In the other he was riding with a gang like Utah Tyrrell's and they hit Holly Town like a hurricane, splitting it wide open, rocking it from one end to the other. Curt wasn't absolutely certain which of the two he wanted more.

"Barney, you find out when Rita's friend is due if you can," Curt said thoughtfully.

"I can find out," Barnaby promised. "But it ain't likely he'd let anybody take him alive, son."

"Well, I don't think I'd want to take him, anyway," Curt said. "But maybe I can talk with him, Barney. Utah could be kind of shorthanded after that Arrowhead show."

When Curt went to bed that night sleep would not come. He was a kid of fifteen again, reliving the shame and horror of a decade ago. He finished the whiskey, but it brought him no relief. He couldn't stop thinking, no matter how hard he fought against it. He had to sweat it out in detail, suffer once more through the appalling and monstrous tragedy that had destroyed the Metheny family.

FIVE

On that night ten years ago, the boys had been playing cavalry and Indians in the lumber yard at the edge of town. But they were getting too old for that game; it seemed more childish than ever since Jack Metheny had run away to join the regular U. S. Cavalry. For Curt, nothing was much fun, nothing seemed right and real and good, now that Jack was gone—and Amanda, too. He was lonely, unhappy, and the situation at home filled him with sick dread.

As they straggled back into Front Street, Curt was detached and silent in the midst of noisy, jubilant companions. Lyme Vector and Stan Russett tried to duck him in the stone watering trough before the town hall, but Curt fought off the bigger boys until Theron Ware and Pat Shannon came to his rescue and broke it up. When Jack was around, no one had bothered Curt, but some of the older kids were beginning to pick on him now. Even in adolescence Lyme Vector had an evil look, mature and knowing beyond his years, and Curt was a bit afraid of him.

They wound up shooting pool at Marr's, on a broken-down table in the side room that the proprietor retained for the youngsters, but Curt Metheny's mind was not on the game. After he missed several easy shots, Lyme Vector began to ride him hard.

"Get off me, Lyme," said Curt, his voice choked and shaky.

Vector laughed in malicious glee and went on baiting the smaller boy. "Don't talk back to me, punk. Your big brother Jack ain't here to back you up. You shoot pool like a girl. Why don't you hang up that cue stick and let the men play?"

"Keep it up," Curt panted, "and you'll get the stick—right in that dirty face."

Vector and Russett roared with mocking laughter. Pat Shannon said, "Lay off the kid, Lyme. He's got enough troubles," but Vector went on with his raw-hiding: "Always wondered what Curt was going to be. Now I know. A professional pool shark. All his family made something of themselves. The old man's the biggest drunk in the Ontawee. Jack was our top lady-killer, and Amanda went off with a two-bit tinhorn—"

Curt Metheny slammed his stick on the table and swung with blind fury at the buck-toothed face of Lyme Vector. A solid shock jarred Curt's left arm, and Vector's head snapped back under the whipping impact. By sheer luck Curt had landed one square in Lyme's eye, and that eye was gashed and swelling purple as Lyme came lunging back toward Curt. The others crowded in between them, forced them apart, and one of

Marr's strong-arm attendants herded them all outside into the dark alley.

Lyme Vector broke loose there and smashed away at Curt's face, the speed and power of his long arms beating down Curt's guard and driving him backward. An adobe wall caught Curt's shoulders and held him upright, stunned and shaken to the heels, the taste of blood like copper in his mouth.

Vector came in to crush and grind him on the wall, but Curt ducked under the sweeping arms and came up inside, lashing left and right at that ugly face, feeling a savage joy as his fists crashed home and rocked Lyme backward. A rain barrel saved Vector from falling. He bounced off it and charged, panting curses and flailing in mad fury. Curt met him head-on, and they fought back and forth from wall to wall. Lyme had the advantage of height, weight, and reach, but he was blind in one eye now, and Curt's hands were quicker and surer, fired with a killing rage that jolted and staggered the bigger boy.

Lyme Vector was losing, getting the worst of it with the fists, when he bulled into a clinch, wrapped his great arms round Curt, and wrestled him to the earth. In this type of combat Curt had no chance. Lyme pinned him securely, grinding him into the dirt and rubble, and punished him with fist, elbow, and knee. Curt was almost out when a man burst through the ring of watching boys, ripped Lyme upright and flung him against a row of ash cans, and lifted Curt to his feet.

It was Barnaby, holding Curt gently and speaking to Vector and the rest with cold, biting scorn: "Twice his size, and you couldn't take him in a fair stand-up fight. If I ever hear of you touching him again, Vector, I'll beat them horse teeth down your throat. And what was you other boys going to do? Stand by and watch that big galoot half kill this kid?"

Nobody, not even Lyme Vector, dared to talk back to Barnaby, and Barney led Curt Metheny out of the alley, helped him brush off his clothes and wash up at the horse trough, and sent him homeward with the words: "You fought real good, Curt—you had him licked. Jack'd be proud of you, and Jud oughta be—and I am. You fought like a Metheny, and nobody can say more than that."

Walking toward home, warmed and uplifted by the tribute from Barnaby, Curt began to feel some pride and satisfaction in the way he had stood up to Lyme Vector. There had been no more fear after it started, and he would never again fear Lyme—or anyone else, large or small. Curt had fought his first real fight alone, without the support of his brother Jack, and from here on he would be ready for any of them.

A group of men at a street corner fell silent as Curt neared them, and he supposed they had been talking about his family. He could feel their eyes on his back after he passed, and he wished he was grown and wearing a gun. *The time'll come,* the boy thought grimly. *I'll make them back down and crawl into their holes, the way Dad and Barney do now.*

He heard his father and mother arguing before he reached the house. Once his heart had gone up at the sight of those lighted windows, but now it sank dismally. Jud was drunk and shouting, and Martha was screaming back at him. The frenzied cries rose higher and louder, and Curt went cold all over. He wanted to turn and run and never come back here, but he walked numbly toward the animal sounds of anger and hatred.

The front door closed behind him, Curt halted tense and trembling in the dim hallway, the voices from the lighted kitchen dinning in his ears.

"That nagging tongue of yours, woman," Jud was roaring. "That blacksnake whip tongue would peel the hide off a bull buffalo. It drove Jack and Amanda away from home, and it's driving me crazy."

"My tongue?" yelled Martha. "I never raised my voice till you began drinking like a maniac. It's drink that's driving you crazy, Jud, and everybody in town knows it. You're the one who drove your son and daughter out of this house. Nobody can live with a drunkard—*nobody!* And I

63

can't stand it any more. I've got to get out of here."

"Go, damn it, go ahead, get out! You're no good to me or anyone else. I know that Zed Parkhurst's been hanging round here again. Well, he's welcome to you. Go on away with that scarecrow of a nester before I kill the both of you."

"You know Zed Parkhurst's nothing but an old friend of my family's. He was engaged to marry one of my sisters once—you know all about that. He comes here as a friend, to help out in time of trouble, and that's all. Don't try to make something dirty of it. Your whiskey-soaked brain twists and spoils everything. You've ruined this family, and you'll put me in my grave before you're done!" Her voice kept rising, until it was a shattering screech. "I'm going to leave you, Jud—I've got to leave you!"

"Shut up, Martha," said Jud in a lower tone, suddenly seeming to regain the composure that was characteristic of him in a normal state. "Please quiet down, Martha; get hold of yourself. We can't fight like this, Martha—it's no good. Take it easy now, please."

"Don't tell me to shut up! You drive me insane, you drunken brute, and then tell me to quiet down. You—Don't hit me, Jud! Don't you dare to hit me!"

"Be still, then, just be still. I don't want to hit you.

Don't make me, Martha." He sounded controlled and reasonable now, but Martha, tortured beyond her limit, could not—or would not—check her shrieking tirade. After more pleas, Jud struck her, the smack of the open-handed blow sounding clearly. Martha's screaming attained greater heights of intensity, and Jud struck again and again until that ear-splitting flow of sound was shut off abruptly and Curt heard the thump of his mother's body on the floor.

Unthinking, his mind as numb as his body, Curt lifted the Henry repeater from its rack and moved trancelike toward the kitchen, levering a shell into the chamber as he went. Martha was sprawled by the table, sobbing silently now, and Jud lowered the whiskey bottle he was drinking from to stare at his son.

"What you going to do with that rifle, Curt?" he asked mildly.

"I—I dunno," the boy said, in honest confusion.

"Curt, I had to hit her. It was the only way to stop that damn screaming. I didn't hit her real hard."

"You—you won't fight any more, will you?"

"No, Curt. We aren't going to fight any more."

Curt tried to swallow the knot in his throat while tears blurred his eyes and trickled down his thin cheeks. "Don't drink—too much, Dad—please."

"I won't, Curt. Just enough to go to sleep on,"

Jud said hoarsely, his own eyes blinking and misted as he knelt beside Martha. "And I'll take care of your mother."

"Get away from me," Martha moaned. "Don't you touch me—not ever again."

Blind with tears, Curt stood the rifle in the corner and turned quickly away. But instead of going upstairs to his room, he opened the front door and stepped out into the night. He had to get out of that house, away from his father and mother. He couldn't sleep under that roof tonight, even though there was no other place to go except the hayloft in the livery barn. And he would not sleep much, wherever he went.

In the morning when Curt went back home with fearful reluctance, his mother was gone and his father was lying unconscious on the bedroom floor. At first Curt thought he was dead, but Jud was only half-dead from drink. The boy fled from the whiskey-reeking room to fetch Doc Pillon.

Barnaby returned to the house with them and stayed with Curt after they got Jud undressed and washed and into bed under drugs. Together Barney and Curt kept house and cared for Jud, who recovered quickly and was remorseful and penitent.

"Where'd Ma go, Dad?" asked Curt when his father awoke to sanity.

"I don't know, Curt," said Jud, with agony in his deep gray eyes. "Maybe to stay with Zed

Parkhurst. He's an old friend of her family's, you know."

"You want me to go after her, Dad?"

"No—not yet, Curt."

"Don't you want her back?"

"Yes, I do," Jud said. "But I'm not sure she'll want to come."

"She'll come," Curt said with assurance. "She won't stay away from us, Dad."

"I hope you're right, son. We'll see after I'm up and around—"

Jud Metheny didn't take a drink for two weeks, and said he was off the stuff for the rest of his life, but something happened to alter that resolve on the day he was starting for Lodestone to see his wife. As Jud came out of the hardware store with a fresh supply of cartridges, a man on the street made a remark about Martha's living with Zed Parkhurst, and Jud struck him one tremendous wallop. It fractured the man's jaw and knocked him clear over a hitch rail into the street. Jud glanced around at the onlookers, turned, and strode into the Ten-High and started drinking whiskey.

He was drunk when he rode out, and he had packed a few bottles in his saddlebags, but it didn't show on him. The newspapers later described him as being "inflamed, unbalanced, and crazed by strong drink," but that was a gross exaggeration. Jud did stop at the house to strap on his old double-sheathed gunbelt and pick up his Henry rifle, and the papers played that up as indicative of premeditation on Jud's part. Whatever it was, it prompted young Curt into saddling up and riding after his father that afternoon. Curt knew where he was going. Parkhurst had a little homestead-ranch layout up near the deserted mining town of Lodestone.

The sun had set and dusk was hazing the prairie with blue and lavender when Curt sat his horse back in the trees and watched his father ride in toward the crude corrals and sheds about the ranch house. It came to Curt as never before what a striking figure Judson Metheny made in the saddle, big and easy, with fine strong features and a clean-limbed grace about him, every movement fluid and flawless.

Jud dismounted in the yard, left his rifle in its scabbard, and turned to the dugout like any visitor on a casual call. A blued steel barrel jutted from a slit in the log facade, and Parkhurst shouted a warning:

"Don't come any closer, Metheny!"

Jud paused, right hand raised in the peace sign, and called back: "I just want to talk to Martha. I got a right to talk to my wife."

An evening breeze carried their voices to Curt in the clump of cottonwoods. He was rigid with fear, waiting for his father to be shot down. He wanted to ride in to Jud's side, but he remained frozen motionless in the leather, more afraid of his father's anger than of Parkhurst's rifle.

"She don't want to see you, Metheny," yelled Parkhurst. "Git back on that horse and ride out."

"She'll see me—if you let her, Park."

"Git outa here before I start shooting. I've got you cold."

"I'm coming in, Park," said Jud Metheny, stepping lightly forward. "Don't do anything foolish, man."

Parkhurst's cry was high-pitched with panic: "Stop right there, Jud! Stop or I'll shoot you dead in your tracks!"

"You don't want to shoot me, Park," said Jud, walking onward in easy-measured strides, empty hands at his sides.

There was a commotion within the dugout, the rifle barrel jerked and vanished behind the logs, and there were sounds of struggling and over-turning furniture. *Ma must've jumped him,* Curt thought as he saw Jud spring forward, gun leaping into his right hand, and ram into the door. Afterward, Curt couldn't be absolutely certain, but it seemed to him there was a muffled explosion inside the cabin before the door gave under Jud's driving shoulder. Then Jud was inside and guns were blasting and roaring. Curt glimpsed bright flashes through the tiny windows and saw smoke curl out the open doorway.

The firing ceased, and stillness was strange and

eerie in the deepening dusk. Racked with dry sobbing, Curt strained to hold his spooked bronc, sure that all three of them must be dead in that dugout. There was no sound from the interior. Powder smoke stained the darkening air and stung Curt's nostrils as he finally reined down the bucking horse.

After a timeless interlude, Judson Metheny came out the door, alone, with bowed head and sagging shoulders, moving like a man in a shocked stupor. Curt longed to join his father then, but something held him back in the shadow of the trees. Jud yanked a bottle from his saddlebags, took a long drink, and swung to the saddle with the bottle still in his big right hand. Flooded with despair and terror, Curt watched him ride slowly away into the purple shadows. He knew he'd never see Dad again—not alive, anyway—and he knew that Ma was already dead behind that log wall.

Curt didn't want to go near the place, but some compulsion urged him toward it. He got down and stumbled to the doorway, the reek of gunsmoke biting at his nose and throat. Zed Parkhurst was sprawled face down over his rifle in the splintered wreckage of a table and chairs. In the corner beyond Martha Metheny lay with blood on her face and dress and the wall behind her. They were both dead.

With a strangled cry Curt turned and fled to his

horse, flung himself into the saddle, and rode out as if all the legions of hell were in pursuit. He had to get to Barnaby. There was no one left but Barney. *Dad didn't kill Ma, I know he didn't,* Curt thought fiercely. *But he'll get the blame for it.*

By noon the next day the story was all over the Ontawee, and posses were being raised in Holly Town and out on the range. Jud Metheny had murdered his wife and Zed Parkhurst. The whole country would soon be up and out after the killer.

Curt told his story to Barnaby, and together they presented the facts to Marshal Ed Gracey and other officials. Curt said Jud had gone to Lodestone to talk things over peaceably with his wife, but Parkhurst had threatened him with a rifle. Jud hadn't even drawn a gun, and Parkhurst was going to shoot him. Martha Metheny tried to prevent this; Parkhurst shot her; and Jud went in and got the man who had killed his wife.

But nobody except Barney believed the boy's version of it. A clear case of double murder was the verdict. The kid, naturally enough, was trying to cover up his father.

Later, another witness came forward with a story similar to Curt's, but this evidence was likewise discredited and ignored. It was old Spider Werle, the hermit of Lodestone, and everyone in the country knew that Spider was crazy as a loon.

So the posses gathered and liquored up and swarmed out on the trace of Jud Metheny. The manhunt was on, the biggest one the Ontawee had ever known. Curt prevailed upon Barnaby to take him along, and they followed Ed Gracey's unit through the Sand Hills into the tortuous, sun-blistered Potholes. There the hunters finally ran down and cornered Jud Metheny, but he refused to surrender and the siege began, with one man fighting off a surrounding army.

A federal marshal, Ed Gracey, the county sheriff, and Barnaby all took a turn at trying to talk Jud into giving himself up, but Jud wouldn't consider it, even for Ed and Barney. "You'll never hang me, boys," came Jud's shouted response, loud and clear over the rocks and sand. "You'll have to come in and shoot me—and I'll get some of you on the way."

Ed Gracey promised Jud safe conduct to jail and a fair trial, but Jud's answer was: "You mean well, Ed, but you can't handle that mob out there. They've already convicted me. So let 'em come and get me."

Curt Metheny tried several times to break away and get through to join his father, but Barnaby always caught the boy and brought him back behind the firing line. "I'd go myself, Curt, if it would help Jud—or do any good at all. But what would one more man—or two—mean against this pack of wolves?"

"Maybe I could get Dad to give up," Curt pleaded.

"No, his mind's set," Barney said. "Jud's going to fight it out to the end."

For thirty-six hours of almost ceaseless combat, Judson Metheny stood off that horde of manhunters, and in that time he killed five posse members and winged a half-dozen others. Then Jud ran out of ammunition, and the ring of gunfire closed in on him.

Jud was unconscious, wounded four times and close to death, when they captured him at last, and he was proved right in his refusal to surrender. Ed Gracey and Barnaby, with the marshal and sheriff and assorted deputies, tried to protect the dying man, but the mob overwhelmed them and strung Jud up on a stunted juniper. Barney got Curt away before the hanging occurred, but the boy's suffering would have been little worse had he witnessed the scene. It was etched indelibly on Curt's mind, as if he had seen it all.

"Jud was out; he didn't know or feel a thing," Barnaby said, in a desperate and honest attempt to console the kid, but Curt was beyond any comfort.

Thus the horror had ended ten years back—but not for Curt Metheny. It would be with him as long as he lived.

SIX

Everything had gone dead wrong and plumb to hell in Arrowhead, Utah Tyrrell was thinking morbidly, as he bound the fresh dressing into place on Spanish's shattered chest, his long-fingered hands graceful, strong, and gentle in the process. Laredo and Wind River had died there in that blazing street—it was a wonder any of them had got out alive. Comanche had been lost somewhere in their wild flight from town. Now Spanish was dying; Old Pitts was hard hit; and most of the others had flesh wounds. Utah himself had been nicked above the left hip. Scarcely more than a burn, but his belt aggravated and chafed it.

"The pain—she won't stop," Spanish panted, dark eyes dilated with agony in his drawn face. "Better you shoot me, Utah—or give me a gun."

"You're going to be all right," Utah lied. "Just hang on, *amigo*."

Spanish tried to smile, his fever-parched lips grimacing on the white teeth. "*La cola del mundo*," he murmured faintly, and Utah smiled down at him. Yes, the tail-end of the world all right, Utah thought bleakly. For you, Spanish, and maybe for all of us. Their luck, which was running so good, had changed, and from here on out it was apt to be all bad. It would be an act of mercy to shoot Spanish, but Utah couldn't do it. Bowden and Goedert would have obliged, but Utah would not let them.

He got up, hitching his gunbelt to ease the raw burning of his side, and moved on to where Old Pitts was bedded down in blood-starched blankets, his face ghastly and sunken under the gray whiskers, his eyes glazed from long suffering.

"How's my boy Spanish, Utah?" asked Pitts.

"Coming along good," Utah said, lying again. "He's going to make it, Orson."

"Well, I ain't," Pitts said stolidly. "Too damn old—and tired. Don't fuss over me none, Utah. Just give me a drink."

"Water?" Utah reached solemnly for his canteen.

"Naw, pain-killer." Orson Pitts grinned and hunched up on his elbows, groaning, to take the pint bottle from Utah's hand. "You know right well what I want." He drank and lay back, his eyes squinting past Utah's shoulder as a shadow fell across them. "Shame to waste good whiskey—ain't it, Bowie?"

Bowie Bowden had come in from lookout to stand over them, lean and tough and limber as a whip-thong, hat cocked at a rakehell angle, thumbs hooked into his gunbelt. His eyes were mean, his mouth was scornful; and there was insolence in every line of him.

"It is for a fact, a damn shame," he agreed.

"Quiet, Bowie," said Utah Tyrrell, with soft-voiced emphasis.

"Utah's human," Old Pitts said. "He ain't all wolf—like you and Herm."

"In this business you can be too human." Bowden laughed and turned away in his lazy swagger. "Pouring good liquor into a dead man, for godsakes!"

"Don't mind Bowie, Orson," said Utah gently.

"I don't mind nothing no more," Pitts said. "But you watch out for him, Utah. He's getting meaner by the minute—him and Herm both."

It was true, Utah Tyrrell realized. Since Arrowhead, everything was different. Bowie and Herm Goedert were beginning to balk against Utah's authority, as if he were wholly to blame for that disaster. Eventually they'd get cocky enough to call him. Utah wasn't worried; he still had Jakes and the Kid and Dusty. But it bothered him to see the outfit splitting up, after all the jobs they had pulled together. It had been a great crew until that fiasco in Arrowhead.

Utah couldn't yet comprehend what had happened at Arrowhead. Something must have leaked out; somebody had talked too much somewhere. But Utah was unable to figure who or where or when. He'd been holding them tight together. Bowie and Herm hadn't been off drinking lately; neither had Kid Ansted and Dusty

Shands. And One-Eyed Jakes hadn't been to see his girl in Holly Town, although that objective was fixed firmly in his mind now.

But something had been spilled, for Arrowhead was ready and waiting for them, the whole town primed and loaded for bear, and they had ridden right into the trap. Utah would never forget that murderous circle of gunfire, lashing and tearing and whipsawing them in front of the Wells Fargo station. Ripping Laredo and Wind River from their saddles, leaving Comanche and Spanish and Old Pitts riddled but still clinging to leather—until Comanche dropped off somewhere along the way out. Utah Tyrrell had thought it was the end, an end he had visualized many times. He marveled that any of them had escaped from that inferno of flame and smoke and screeching lead.

Now Bowie Bowden had paused to stand over Spanish and ask mockingly, "You going to be ready for another all-night ride, Mex? We got to make better time tonight."

"Is nothing to me," Spanish said. "I go—I stay. Whatever Utah wants. *Es nada, nada.*"

"You got more sense than Utah has, Mex," said Bowie. "If it wasn't for you and Old Pitts, we'd be long gone by now, free and clear."

Kid Ansted had come into the clearing, slim and boyish with blond hair and blue eyes, quickening his stride as he saw Bowden standing over Spanish, obviously taunting the wounded man.

"Lay off of him, Bowie," said the Kid, his tone as disgusted as his expression, his right hand spread near the gun that looked oversized on his slender flank.

Bowden smiled at him with casual scorn. "You want trouble with me, Kid? Keep asking for it, sonny, and you're bound to get it."

"You don't scare me, Bowie," said Kid Ansted. "Just leave Spanish and Pitts alone."

Dusty Shands emerged from the brush, stocky, bow-legged, and grinning his homely grin, to take an indolent stance beside the Kid. "You don't scare nobody, Bowie—not even the wounded," Shands said.

Bowden regarded them both. "Keep on, you two young buckos." He laughed with light disdain. "Just keep asking—"

The voice of Utah Tyrrell cut in, still mild but carrying a thin edge of steel: "Break it up, boys, and get back on watch. We don't want those posses closing up on us."

"They're miles behind, Utah," protested Bowden, turning to him. "All we've seen for days is their far-off dust."

"Let's keep it that way," said Utah.

Bowden stalked away, grumbling under his breath, and Kid Ansted and Dusty Shands separated to make their way to diverse vantage points on the wooded hilltop where they had taken refuge for the daylight hours. Hiding out by day and riding at night, they had been traveling slowly across the high country in a southerly direction, the distant dust of pursuers forcing them gradually toward the Ontawee Valley and Holly Town. Sometimes Utah wondered why the pursuit hadn't caught up with them. Maybe the posse men weren't too eager to overtake this band of gun fighters.

But even with the manhunters lagging, our situation is sorry enough, thought Utah Tyrrell. *We've been in plenty of tight spots before, but never as bad as this one. The whole country aroused and out after us. Two wounded men on our hands, the horses tired and spent, grub and ammunition and money running out. Arrowhead was going to be our last job—for a while, at least—and we didn't get a nickel there. We were going to quit after that one, split the take, and break up and scatter. Now we've got to pull one more job to get something to live on. One more substantial haul before we can do anything. Anything but run and hide, hide and run.*

Utah Tyrrell was a big, rangy man, poised and sure in every move he made, with an easy power flowing in him. Save for the purplish birthmark that covered one side of his fine face, he would have been strikingly handsome. That had been Utah's curse from the beginning.

Employers had been reluctant to hire him, and quick to fire him if anything went wrong. He was bad luck, they declared, the stamp of it plain and shocking on his features. Folks did not want him around, and the sensitive Utah withdrew more and more into himself. The birthmark often prompted remarks that led to fighting and gunplay, and Utah was quick and sure and deadly with a Colt or a Winchester. Once the brand of killer was on him, Utah Tyrrell began to move outside the law, and soon gathered other foot-loose and rejected drifters about him. He had a natural charm, a pleasant manner, that drew and held people when they got to know him. He was a born leader.

The Tyrrell gang had become the scourge of the countryside, holding up banks and stagecoaches and trains, running off cattle and horse herds, striking and vanishing with lightning swiftness. And they were credited with many robberies and killings in which they had no part. This all added to the legend. Nobody could stop them, or come close to catching them, until they rode into that gun-trap in Arrowhead.

Now Utah had a chilling premonition of disaster, a sinking sense of impending death. Their luck had begun to run out, along with everything else. The outfit was beginning to split down the middle, Bowie Bowden and Herm Goedert on one side, Kid Ansted and Dusty Shands on the other, and One-Eyed Jakes standing aloof and indifferent as ever.

Utah sauntered toward the rope corral, in which One-Eyed Jakes was working with patient care on the horses. Utah liked this man, trusted and respected him, but it was impossible to get close to Jakes, to know him. Jakes was tall and trim, nearly as big as Utah, but cut on more slender lines, a man who somehow managed to look clean, even after scorching days and sleepless nights on the trail. The black patch over the right eye gave his carved, stony features a sinister aspect, and there was a bitter grimness in the keen left eye and about the wide mouth. A good-looking boy, except for that patch, with something distinctive in him. It wasn't difficult to understand why a woman in Holly Town, a lovely girl like Rita Corday, would wait for Jakes, and Utah felt a pang of envy and loneliness. There was no one waiting anywhere for Utah Tyrrell.

"You spend a lot of time with them, Jakes," he said.

"It pays off, Utah," said Jakes, glancing up from the bronc he was rubbing down. "And I like horses. More than I like most people."

Utah nodded and smiled understandingly. "You've got something there. Are they in pretty good shape?"

"Considering what they been through. I'm getting rid of the saddle sores Bowie and Herm worked up, and the lameness the Kid's buckskin had. They'll carry us a long way yet."

"We're getting close to Holly. I guess you'll be riding in there one of these nights."

Jakes smiled dimly. "Well, it's been a long time, Utah. I'm due there this week."

"You'll make it, Jakes. And I don't blame you. Rita's a real nice woman. What about that bank in Holly? We're beginning to hurt for money and supplies."

"It's a rich one, Utah," said Jakes, "and nobody's ever hit it that I know of."

"Sounds like a good deal. See what you can find out when you're in town, Jakes. You know our man there?"

"I've picked up messages from him at the Mustang. Never saw him."

"Try to get in touch with him this time," Utah suggested. "We've got to strike something pretty soon."

Jakes nodded solemnly. "Can I start tonight, Utah?"

"I think maybe you'd better."

"Bowie and Herm aren't going to like it much."

Utah laughed softly. "They don't like anything much. But they'll have to hold still for it. Or get out."

"If we weren't shorthanded, Utah, I'd say let 'em go."

"Me too. But we'll need 'em for this job."

The crackle of brush and crunch of boots brought them both around, to watch Herm

82

Goedert come in from his outpost, a giant with an ugly, scowling face.

"Nothing but dust off in the hills," Goedert announced raspingly. "They couldn't track down a herd of buffalo, them stupid cowpokes." Goedert spat a stream of tobacco juice and glared critically at Jakes. "You still nursing them crow-bait critters, One-Eye?"

Jakes's cold stare fixed on the sullen face of the hulking brute. "If you and Bowie knew how to treat horses, it wouldn't take so long to get 'em in shape."

Herm Goedert snorted and turned to gaze at the two wounded men, his scowl increasing at the sound of their labored breathing. "Ain't they ever going to die? How much longer we got to cart their carcasses round the country? No wonder we can't shake them posses off our tail."

"Quit crying, Herm," said Utah Tyrrell. "They're the ones suffering."

"When we going to get some more grub and whiskey and shells?" demanded Goedert.

"Jakes is heading for Holly tonight."

"He is, huh? Does Bowie know about that?"

"Bowie's got nothing to say about it," Utah told him. "Neither have you, Herm. We figure on taking that bank in Holly Town."

Herm Goedert guffawed. "Sure, Jakes'll learn a whole lot about the bank in the Mustang, won't he, huh?"

Jakes turned from the horses, ducked through the ropes, and strode toward Goedert, his one eye aflame, his voice a cutting whiplash: "Watch that tongue of yours!"

Goedert lumbered backward, snarling, levering a shell into the chamber of his carbine. He lined the barrel at Jakes, who came on in slow, steady strides.

"That's far enough, boys." Utah Tyrrell stepped forward between them and slapped the carbine aside. "We've got the whole outside world to fight; we don't have to fight among ourselves. Herm, get back on lookout. And stay there until I call you in."

Jakes had halted, still ready to draw, and Herm Goedert wheeled away to move ponderously off through the brush and timber of the flat hilltop. Utah sighed wearily.

"Ever since Arrowhead, nothing but trouble. Don't know if I can hold 'em together long enough for one more job."

"They'll stick, Utah," said One-Eyed Jakes. "They're as broke as we are. And they need us more than we need them."

Utah Tyrrell took off his hat and shook his shapely dark head, now streaked and threaded with premature gray. "I don't know, Jakes. Since that night in Arrowhead I've had a queer feeling—The cards aren't coming our way any more."

"That bank in Holly will fix us up again," Jakes said reassuringly. "We'll be all set after that one, Utah. The last one—for me."

"You and Rita going to get married?"

Jakes nodded, a smile softening his chiseled features. "Yes—she's been waiting way too long already."

"This'll be the last one for me too—I hope. But I don't know what I'll do afterward—"

The hot afternoon wore away. Jakes finished grooming the horses and rigging the harnesses he had devised to support and hold Spanish and Old Pitts in their saddles. Then he kindled a tiny fire to heat water for shaving. Utah cared for the wounded, keeping insects off them, trying to comfort and cheer them. Spanish's breathing was a moaning rasp, bubbly at times, and Old Pitts wheezed like a wind-broken bronc.

The outposts reported in at intervals, and Bowie Bowden had his say about Jakes's proposed trip to Holly:

"Crazy to let him go, Utah. He won't come back, and he's liable to talk in there. It was saloon gossip that got us shot up in Arrowhead."

"He's going, Bowie—and he'll come back," Utah Tyrrell said with calm conviction. "I don't worry about Jakes."

Bowden gestured angrily at the wounded pair. "We going to lug them along some more?"

"We can't leave 'em here to die."

Bowden cursed. "They'll die anyway, damn it! And get us all killed in the bargain if they don't hurry up."

"Put yourself in their place," Utah said. "It could've been you or me or any of us."

"I'd shoot myself—like Spanish wants to," Bowie said. "Why the hell don't you give him a gun?"

"Go on back to your place, Bowie," said Utah Tyrrell, with icy finality.

Toward evening Utah went out to relieve Shands so Dusty could go in and prepare a meager supper. Orson Pitts had done the cooking when he was able, and Dusty had learned sketchily from the old man. Now there wasn't much to do it with, anyway. A little bacon and jerked beef, dried biscuits, hardtack, and coffee, a few cans of tomatoes and pears. The whiskey was running low, too, and Bowie and Herm were outraged over Utah's wasting it on two corpses. They had pooled funds for the provisions Jakes was to bring back from Holly Town, and he promised to include a supply of liquor.

They were finishing supper in the cool blue twilight when a muffled explosion brought every man upright with gun in hand. Running in the direction of the wounded men, Utah Tyrrell saw Old Pitts rear up in his blankets and stare at the shrouded figure of Spanish, from which thin coils of smoke were spiraling upward.

"The boy shot himself," Pitts panted. "Who gave him a gun, Utah?"

"I don't know, Orson," said Utah dully. "But Spanish is a lot better off."

"Figured you was lying about him before," Old Pitts muttered, sinking back onto his shoulders with a stifled groan. "Heard men dying in my time, Utah. Well, you only got one dead man to tote around now."

Across the embers of the cook fire, Kid Ansted and Dusty Shands were facing Bowden and Goedert, the ruddy glow staining their taut faces, their pistols in hand but not cocked or lined.

"One of you gave Spanish a gun," the Kid said flatly. "Which one of you was it?"

Utah Tyrrell returned to the fireside and spoke sharply: "Never mind, Kid. Put those guns away, all of you. Spanish didn't have a chance, anyway. I was tempted to slip him a gun myself."

Herm Goedert grinned, "How about the old man? He ain't got a chance neither."

"Leave Pitts alone," Utah said, "or I'll use a gun on you, Herm. Now you and Bowie can start digging a grave. You're the ones who wanted to put Spanish under."

They left Spanish buried in a shallow rock-cairned grave on the forested hilltop and moved out in the early darkness. Old Pitts, tied securely on his horse, was groaning through clenched teeth, and One-Eyed Jakes was leading Spanish's mount to pack provisions on when he reached Holly.

Gaunted and trail-worn, filthy with dust, sweat, and blood, bristling with weapons and draped with extra bandoleers of cartridges, they were a grim, tough-looking crew, the mark of hunted men on them. Picking their way with care, keening the night air around them, they filed through the woodland aisles with equipment jangling. It was slow work, made even slower by the presence of Pitts, and Bowie and Herm railed constantly at their dragging pace. The cry of coyotes sounded from afar, weird and mournful under the vast night-blue sky.

A game trace led them to a cattle run, which in turn took them to a remote overgrown wagon road. In the blackness before moonrise they paused to rest and then went plodding onward in the welcome silvery light of the moon. One-Eyed Jakes took his leave and jogged on ahead of the column to cut away for Holly Town.

"That's the last we'll see of that one-eyed joker," predicted Bowie Bowden sourly. "He'd be a damn fool to leave his girl and come back to this crippled-up outfit."

"I'll lay you two-to-one Jakes'll come back," said Kid Ansted.

"What you going to use for money, Kid?" laughed Bowden.

"We'll have plenty of money after we stand up

that bank in Holly," said Dusty Shands. "That oughta be the biggest one we ever cracked."

"Unless we run into something like we done at Arrowhead," said Herm Goedert. "Maybe our luck's gone."

"One-Eye's ain't gone," Bowie said bitterly. "Imagine being in a nice place like the Mustang with a woman like that redheaded Rita and all the booze you can drink. Sure, Jakes'll crawl out of a nest like that to come back here!"

"I say he will," insisted Kid Ansted, boyish face set hard.

"What the hell do you know about it?" Bowden jeered. "An unweaned calf like you."

"Spanish is the lucky one," Old Pitts mumbled, choking back a moan.

"Cheer up, old man," laughed Herm Goedert. "You'll be with him before long—as lucky as he is."

Alone at the head of the column, Utah Tyrrell found himself sweating in the cool night. The present offered enough problems, and the future was black and desolate. He was responsible for six other men, as well as himself, and the burden of command had never been light on him.

Dear God, he thought prayerfully. *One more job in Holly. Let it be a good one, let it go right, let us all come through alive. Then we'll pull out, try again to go straight and honest.*

SEVEN

On Front Street in the summer evening, Curt Metheny was as isolated as a man can be on a thronged thoroughfare. Women passed him with lifted eyes and chins. Men looked straight through him or obliquely past him. The few that spoke did so furtively or grudgingly; they might as well have remained silent as far as Curt was concerned. This treatment was familiar, but it never failed to hurt and rankle. At times it set him afire with murderous fury. It wasn't pleasant to be a leprous outcast in the town where you were born and raised.

Curt was watchful and wary as he trod the warped boards of the sidewalk. Frying Pan was in town tonight, he understood, and some of the Forbes hands might make a play. Theron Ware had come out of hiding today, although his face looked so bad that J. A. Cottrell had sent him home from the bank. And according to Barnaby, this was the night One-Eyed Jakes was coming in to the Mustang.

The moon was nearing the full, and the stars glittered large and low in the clear sky. The night air was soft and feathery, soothing as balm, and even in town it smelled sweet and fresh. Curt felt a deep loneliness, sharpened by vague, nameless longings. His family had died; his world had crumbled to ashes; and at twenty-five he was old and bitter, alone and defeated. Many men in his predicament became outlaws; there was little else left for them.

On the veranda of the Stockmen's Hotel, Lenora Forbes lounged upon the railing, her slim straight back against an upright. The pose was unconsciously provocative, and emotion welled up in Curt as he saw her. A profiled bosom thrust high in the white shirt, and the skirt of the riding habit was taut on her hip and thigh. She motioned to Curt, and he left the walk to stand below her, aware of people turning curious glances upon them.

"I have to see you, Curt," whispered Lenora. "Where can we meet?"

He pondered briefly. "Out by the river, in back of the livery."

"All right. I'll be there in about fifteen minutes."

"See you then." Curt tipped his hat and went on down the street, feeling alive once more with something to look forward to.

Well past the hotel, Curt turned into an alley and cut across back lots toward the trees that fringed the Ontawee River. There was a ford almost directly behind the livery stable, where the shallow water rippled in silver wavelets under the moon, and the cottonwoods, salt cedars, and willows laid deep shadows along the shore.

After a few minutes of waiting, Curt saw Lenora Forbes crossing the plain with lissome ease, and he moved to meet her. She held out both hands, and Curt took them in his own. A strong current flowed into their arms and bodies as they stood there under the lacy boughs. Her eyes shone darkly up at him, and her perfume sweetened the clean odor of grass and leaves, ferns and running water.

"They're holding a conference in our hotel suite," Lenora said. "Father and Doyle, Lyme and Harry and Theron. It's about you, Curt. What they're going to do—to get rid of you."

"I expected that, Len. Why don't Hooper just turn Lyme and Harry loose on me?"

"No, it won't be that way. They're afraid of Ed Gracey. He's one man they can't control."

"They'll get around the law some way," Curt Metheny said. "The whole town will back them. I just wish they'd start it—and get it done with."

"Theron will probably want to hire a gunman."

Curt nodded. "That's about his style, Lenny."

"Oh, Curt, I'm afraid—afraid for you." Lenora moved in close, her arms locking round his lean waist, and Curt held her with gentle firmness, her dark hair rich and fragrant under his mouth.

"What about Theron?" he asked half tauntingly.

"Since that day at the waterhole, I can't stand Theron Ware."

"Then you aren't engaged to him—any more?"

"I—I haven't broken it—formally," Lenora Forbes said uncertainly. "But it's broken, as far as I'm concerned."

Curt smiled and shook his head. "They won't let you break it."

Lenora looked up at him, searching and suspicious. "Perhaps you don't *want* it broken, Curt. Maybe you don't want me—"

"I want you, all right," he said. "I've always wanted you, Len."

"Nobody else—ever?"

"That's right. No one but you."

She stiffened in his arms. "Not even Rita Corday?"

Curt laughed softly. "She was Jack's girl. She always will be, in my book. She's like a sister to me, Lenny."

"You meet her—up in Lodestone."

"Once, by accident," Curt Metheny murmured. "I guess Stan Russett's been talking to you, Len."

Lenora inclined her head, a trifle sheepish, and Curt told her about the night in Lodestone.

"All right, Curt, I'm sorry—" Lenora lifted her face to his, arms tightening with hungry strength, and Curt crushed her to him as their lips met and held for long, silent moments.

Foreign sounds finally penetrated Curt's reeling senses. Awed, breathless, and shaken, he released the girl and stared through the trees at the ford. The splash of hoofs and creak of saddle gear came plainly now, and moonlight silhouetted a tall horseman crossing the stream in their direction with a pack animal on lead.

"What is it, Curt?" asked Lenora. "Who's coming?"

"A stranger, Len," said Curt, with some relief. "Maybe one of Utah Tyrrell's men. Yes, it is—see that eye patch. It's the one they call One-Eyed Jakes."

"What's he coming to Holly for?"

"To get supplies—and see a girl."

"A girl? What girl?"

"I don't know," Curt said, unwilling to admit that Rita was no longer faithful to his dead brother. *Faithful,* he thought. *A strange word to use in relation to a woman of Rita's reputation. Yet in this case it fitted, it was proper and right.* "Some girl at the Mustang, as the story goes."

"Do men fall in love with—women like that?"

"Sure, sometimes. They marry them, too." Curt was somewhat irritated and resentful. "They're human, after all."

"Well, I suppose so," Lenora said dubiously, and once more the spell between them was broken, the magical moment lost.

The rider had reached the near shore line now, his mount grunting as he climbed the sloping bank, the packhorse following with less difficulty. The outlaw was a high, clean-shouldered shape against the starry heavens, easy and sure as he rode on toward the lights of Holly Town, and Curt Metheny watched him with admiration and something akin to envy.

"A great gun fighter," Curt remarked, almost reverently.

"Isn't he taking an awful chance coming in here?" Lenora asked.

"Wherever they go they're taking a chance, Len."

There was something faintly familiar about the man's figure and bearing, Curt thought, and then it came to him. Jakes had the same look, the same ease and economy of motion, that Curt had seen in his father that dusky afternoon he had ridden into the Parkhurst homestead. Maybe One-Eyed Jakes also was riding to his death.

Curt tried to pull Lenora close again, but she resisted now, struggling against his arms. "No, Curt! I've got to get back to the hotel. They'll start hunting for me if I don't."

"All right," Curt said, biting down on the swear words he felt coming. "You go just so far, Len— then you cut out. With most men it would be too far, girl."

Lenora's laugh was a shade guilty and uneasy. "I don't go that far with anyone but you."

"You'd better not," he said grimly. "If you know what's good for you."

Lenora smiled and stroked his arm. "You never say you love me any more, Curt."

"How can I? When you're promised to Theron."

"But I'm not promised—to anybody. Do you love me, darling?"

"Yes, damn it—I love you, Len."

She laughed in quiet delight. "What a tender, romantic way to put it! One more kiss, Curt—a nice gentle one—and then I must go."

His kiss was cool, quick, and light, and he withdrew when her mouth started clinging to hold him. "You—you devil," she panted softly, looking up at him with shining eyes and trembling lips. "I love you—damn it—I love you, Curt Metheny."

They were emerging from the trees, when a horseman came racking across the flats toward them, a rider tall enough to be Lyme Vector or Theron Ware. Stepping clear of the girl, Curt drew his gun and waited. The showdown might begin right here and now. But it was only Stan Russett, reining up with a flourish and staring down at them as he quieted the prancing black. Curt holstered his Colt.

"So it's you two," Russett said, with a jeering laugh. "A picture that Hooper and Theron ought to see. Curt, you're always skulking round in the bushes with some gal. What is it gets them? That stable smell?"

"It's something you haven't got, Deputy," said Curt.

"It's a stink I don't want, stableboy."

"Get down and say that again, Stanko."

Stan Russett rocked in his saddle with laughter, exulting in the advantage a rider enjoys over a man on foot. "I don't have to get down. I can smell you from here."

"Beat it, Stanko," said Curt Metheny. "Before I blow you off that black show horse."

"That's all you need to do in this town—throw a gun on a lawman."

"You're a lawman? No wonder the law's a joke. On your way, Stanko."

Russett glanced from Curt to Lenora with a lecherous wink. "Sorry if I interrupted something out here—"

Curt lunged forward at that. Russett drove the horse at him, and Curt sprang aside, but the heavy-muscled shoulder of the black struck him. Spinning away from the jarring impact, Curt got his boots tangled in the grass and tripped into a sidewise tumble. Russett wheeled the horse about and reared high above Curt, trying to force the beast to trample him, but Curt flipped and rolled swiftly away from under the hoofs.

Coming catlike to his feet with gun in hand, Curt said, "Get going, Stanko, before I kill you."

His stern features blanched and crumpling, Stan Russett yanked the black around and spurred off at a run for town. Curt was about to throw a shot after him when Lenora Forbes hauled down his gun-hand.

"Don't fire, Curt. That's just what he wants you to do. Let the stupid lout go. You can't take that clown serious. He isn't worth wasting a thought on."

"You're right, Lenny," panted Curt. "But one of these days I'll have to cut him down."

"He's nothing, Curt. Less than nothing. Forget about him."

They paused to say good night at the edge of the plain outside town, and Lenora Forbes said anxiously, "Watch yourself, Curt. Stan'll run and tell my father and Theron. They may try something tonight."

"Yeah, I'll be on the lookout, Len."

"Where you going now?"

"To meet Barney at the livery," Curt said. "Later, I'm going to try and see One-Eyed Jakes. Maybe he'll take me back to Utah's bunch with him."

Lenora's dark eyes widened at him. "You want to go with *them?*"

"I've got to get away from here, go somewhere, Lenny. Before they frame me—or kill me. You know how things are in Holly."

"Yes, Curt, I know," Lenora murmured sadly. "I don't want you to go—don't want you to be an outlaw. But you might be safer and better off with them than you are here. No matter what happens, Curt, you'll come back to me, won't you?"

"I'll come back to you, Lenny," he promised.

"Most likely I won't get out of town, anyway. But it's worth a try."

Lenora's eyes were shimmering wet, and Curt tasted the tears in their farewell kiss. "Good luck and God bless you, my love," she said, husky with sorrow. "And be careful, please be careful."

"Don't worry, I'll be all right, Len. Don't you let them drive you back to Theron."

"I—I won't. I'll try, Curt. Probably have to go to the dance with him Saturday, but that won't mean anything."

Curt smiled at her. "It better not, baby. You're my gal."

"And you're my boy—always." Lenora smiled through the tears as she moved away in the direction of the hotel, and Curt's eyes were stinging as he watched her go slim and girlish with that ripe womanly depth and fullness at breast and hip, her dark head erect, her stride free, strong and graceful.

Those were high hopes they shared, but somehow Curt Metheny didn't fully believe they would ever come true. There were too many men, too many guns, standing between them.

Curt walked toward the rear of the livery barn, thinking ironically that the outlaw, One-Eyed Jakes, was in no more danger in Holly tonight than Curt himself was—and perhaps even less.

EIGHT

In the parlor of his year-round suite at the Stockmen's Hotel, Hooper Forbes was presiding over an informal gathering. The room was furnished with opulent luxury, lamplight from a crystal chandelier spilling over brocaded drapes, thick carpets, plush chairs, and carved tables. Hooper maintained the suite for the convenience of his family and friends, and to accommodate guests from the East or from other great ranches. Hooper and Theron Ware were at home in this setting, but the other three men, booted, spurred, and gun-hung, looked out of place and uncomfortable.

Relaxed in his favorite chair, Hooper Forbes was eating chocolate candies from a cut-glass dish. At his right, Theron Ware reclined at ease on the overstuffed sofa, an elegant figure in spite of his bruised and swollen face. The mustache partially concealed the cut-puffed mouth, but nothing could hide the humped crookedness of his once-straight nose. At Hooper's left, Doyle Guinness sat stiffly in another easy chair, chewing on a cigar, holding a whiskey glass, and looking fretful and impatient. Across the table from them in straight-backed chairs, Lyme Vector and Harry Keech were smoking cigars and drinking whiskey at a rate that caused Hooper to frown with displeasure.

"You boys drink too much," Hooper said testily, sucking the cream filling from another chocolate and smacking his flabby lips.

"Working men git thirsty," Harry Keech said with a loose grin.

"Your liquor's too good to resist, Hoop," said Lyme Vector, buck teeth bared under his beaked nose. "But let's get to the business at hand if you're so worried about this bottle."

Hooper Forbes grunted. "I got more whiskey than you two hogs could ever guzzle. Now, Theron, what's on your mind?"

"I guess we all know—it's Curt Metheny," said Theron Ware, examining the ash on his cigar. "Since that afternoon at South Waterhole, I can't do anything with Lenora, can't get anywhere near the girl. You've noticed the change in her, Hooper. Curt's poisoned her mind against all of us."

"That's the truth," Forbes admitted. "I can't reach Lenora myself. She won't hardly speak to me. She always had a weakness for that Metheny mongrel."

"Love goes where it's sent," Doyle Guinness put in gruffly. "Even you can't control something like that, Hoop. You can't stop the girl from wanting Metheny."

"I can get rid of Metheny, by God!" boomed Hooper Forbes.

"Sure, Hoop, that ain't no problem," Lyme

Vector said carelessly. "I'll take Curt any time you say the word."

"Ed Gracey wouldn't stand for it, Lyme," said Forbes. "Ed's getting too old and crochety—and too big for his britches. We need a new town marshal here, and we're going to have one right soon."

"Stan Russett would make us a good man," Theron Ware declared. "Stan's sensible, he'll listen to reason; but you can't talk to Gracey." Languidly, he polished his nails on the lapel of his coat.

"Gracey's bullheaded and mule-stubborn," agreed Forbes. "And he's been in office too long."

"He's still a good marshal, Hoop," said Doyle Guinness. "One of the best lawmen I ever saw."

Lyme Vector laughed disparagingly. "Ed's gone a long ways on that old gun-slinging rep of his. He don't worry me none, Hoop."

"He's the law here," Hooper Forbes said flatly. "Until we get that badge off him—There ought to be some other way of handling young Metheny."

"Couldn't we make it look like an accident?" Harry Keech queried. "Seems like we could if we give it some thought. Curt could fall outa that hayloft in the livery, or git beat to death in some dark alley when he's drunk. He gits drunk enough."

"That's a possibility," Forbes said. "We might put some thought on that, boys."

Harry Keech bowed to Lyme Vector, and poured two more drinks.

"Why not hire a gunman from outside?" Theron Ware suggested. "It'd be quick, clean, and easy that way, and nobody could tie us to it."

"Not much!" scoffed Lyme Vector. "Everybody'd know damn well who was behind it, and Ed Gracey'd be the first to know. I still say let me take him. I owe Curt something on my old man."

"So do I," murmured Theron Ware. "But I can't afford to get involved in any shooting scrape."

"None of us can, Theron," said Hooper Forbes, reaching for a glass of water to wash down the sweets. "We got to figure a better way than that."

"We might get one of those killers from the Tyrrell gang," Ware remarked thoughtfully.

Doyle Guinness chuckled. "There's ten posses out hunting them. How you going to make connections there?"

"I've heard that one of them comes in here to the Mustang."

Hooper Forbes coughed and water ran down his fat jowls. "The Mustang! That's another thing I want rubbed out, by the Almighty! The Mustang and them other places are a living disgrace to this community. They ought to be shut down and run out of town."

"I agree with you, Hooper," said Theron Ware. "I've told Gracey time and again to clamp down on those places. But Ed claims a frontier town needs joints like that."

Lyme Vector and Harry Keech winked, nudged one another, and broke out laughing at this. Doyle Guinness fingered his gray mustache and drawled with sly malice: "You sure you wouldn't miss them spots any, Theron?"

"What are you talking about?" Ware demanded with righteous indignation, glaring from Guinness to Vector and Keech.

Hooper Forbes pounded the table with a hamlike fist. "Let's get back to business here. What we going to do about Curt Metheny?"

Lyme Vector swished whiskey around in his mouth and swallowed pleasurably. "Turn me loose, Hoop, and I'll burn him down for you."

"Come Saturday night, Curt'll be good and drunk," Harry Keech said. "If they find him dead in an alley, who the hell's going to care?"

"Ed Gracey, for one," Hooper Forbes said gloomily.

"And Lenora, for another," Doyle Guinness added.

Forbes scowled at his foreman. "She'll get over it, Doyle—women always do. But I want you boys to lay off Curt—for the time being. There must be smarter ways."

"Sure like to get hold of that big gray horse of Curt's," mused Doyle Guinness absently. "That's one helluva lot of horse."

Theron Ware got up to pace the floor, impatient and restless. "I'll think of something, Hooper. Leave it to me—for now."

Doyle Guinness blew smoke through his stained mustache. "What's all the fuss and feathers about, anyway? You're making a mountain out of a molehill. Give Curt time and he'll get himself killed—it's in the cards, pure and simple. Curt Metheny ain't meant to live long."

"There's young Alvah Parkhurst, who fancies himself a gun sharp," Harry Keech put in. "He goes round bragging that he'll shoot Curt on sight. He'll git to Curt sooner or later."

"I'll see that somebody does," Theron Ware said. "By Saturday night, at the latest. Shall we leave it like that?" He looked at the gold watch J. A. Cottrell had given him.

"Might as well, I guess," Hooper Forbes grumbled. "These boys have emptied my bottle, so they're probably ready to drift. You riding home with me and Lenora, Doyle?"

Guinness inclined his gray head. "Must be too drunk to go anywhere else, Hoop, according to your standards."

Forbes eyed Keech and Vector. "Don't make any damn-fool play now."

The meeting adjourned with Theron Ware going to his own room at the rear of the hotel, while the others descended to the lobby. Stan Russett met them there, and addressed himself to the rancher:

"I just run across Lenora with Curt Metheny, out by the river."

"You did, huh?" Forbes said heavily, his broad face darkening. "Well, what about it?"

"I—I was going to bring Lenora in, but Curt threatened me with his gun."

"Why didn't you arrest him?" Forbes demanded.

"He—he had the drop on me," Russett stammered, flushing red beneath his tan.

Hooper Forbes snorted in disgust. "So what do you want me to do?"

"I—I thought—you didn't want Lenora with—him."

"I don't," Forbes said. "But apparently I can't keep her away from him."

"You—you want him arrested now?" Russett floundered.

"What for? Talking to my daughter?" Hooper Forbes asked with caustic sarcasm, while Vector and Keech burst into immoderate laughter, and Guinness no longer tried to conceal his contemptuous grin.

Stan Russett drew himself up tall and rigid. "All right. Sorry I bothered you." He turned and marched out the front door, followed by the laughter of all four men.

"He's the one Theron wants for town marshal?" Doyle Guinness said incredulously, shaking his grizzled head.

Lyme Vector sobered and turned to Forbes.

"You want us to go after Metheny tonight, Hoop?"

Forbes frowned in thoughtful consideration. "No—not yet, Lyme. Unless you catch him all alone, with no witnesses—"

Theron Ware had settled down in his own modest quarters to wait for the others to go their various ways so he could slip down to the Mustang. He had to get there tonight, regardless of his reputation, and not entirely for the purpose that generally lured him in that direction.

This was the night that the outlaw from Utah Tyrrell's band was supposed to pay Rita Corday a visit, so he had heard. It figured to be right, because Rita hadn't worked all week, which was an almost certain sign that she was expecting the notorious One-Eyed Jakes.

A plan had been formulating in Ware's brain throughout the conference in the Forbes suite, but it was not one he wished to share with anybody. After that Arrowhead deal blew up in their faces, the bandits must be desperate for money. For a few hundred dollars, at the most, he could get One-Eyed Jakes to put Curt Metheny under. A reasonable enough assumption. What was one more victim to a killer like Jakes? Theron smiled serenely at the utter simplicity of it.

He would pay Jakes one-half the fee in advance, and the balance after Curt Metheny was dead. When Jakes came after the final payment,

Theron would shoot him down, retrieve his own money, or turn him over to Marshal Ed Gracey for the reward. As near as Theron could recall, there was at least two thousand dollars on Jakes's head, and possibly more. A neat means of getting rid of Curt Metheny, making a hero of himself, and adding a couple of thousand to his bank account.

And with Curt Metheny out of the way, Theron would have a clear field with Lenora Forbes. For some incomprehensible reason, Lenora seemed to prefer Curt to himself. Theron couldn't understand such a gross lack of discrimination, but he supposed it was one of those feminine foibles that made the sex so unfathomable. But once Curt was dead and gone, Lenora would soon get over him and turn back to Theron Ware.

Theron would have liked to do the killing himself, but he had his position in the bank and the community to consider. Old J. A. Cottrell was about ready to promote him to the office of treasurer, but he'd never do it if Theron got mixed up in any gunplay. J. A. insisted that a banker's conduct should always be above reproach.

If the plot to use One-Eyed Jakes didn't pan out, through some unforeseen freak of fortune, there were other methods. There were always gunhands to be hired. And there was young Alvah Parkhurst. Parkhurst was forever threatening to get Curt Metheny. A little money, liquor, and encouragement would certainly trigger the Parkhurst kid into action, because he was hell-bent on winning renown as a gun fighter.

But One-Eyed Jakes was the first bet—and by far the best one. He was a true professional.

At the mirror Theron combed and brushed his long black hair with fastidious care. The sight of his misshapen nose and welted cheekbones left him grimacing as he adjusted the black string tie and white collar and set the tailored coat on his broad shoulders. Curt had ruined his looks, but he'd pay for it—with his life. *I should've let Lyme drag him to death that afternoon,* Theron reflected. *But I wanted to beat the life out of him with my own hands. And I would have, too, if Lenora hadn't butted in with that gun of Curt's.*

Setting the white hat aslant on his burnished head and patting the shoulder-holstered pistol under his left armpit, Theron Ware left the room and took the rear stairway, to circle and cut across backlot areas toward the row of houses on the outskirts. He'd have to catch One-Eyed Jakes when he was leaving the Mustang, for it wouldn't do to let Rita Corday know anything about it. Rita was strangely devoted to Curt Metheny. Theron wondered what there was about Curt that made women like him so much. He wasn't as good-looking or well-dressed or socially prominent as Theron Ware. Curt was nothing but a manure-shoveling hostler in the livery barn, whereas

Theron was an up-and-coming official in the bank. Yet the girls seemed to go for Curt Metheny. Rita Corday refused to have anything to do with him. She never had liked him, and it was one of the things that rankled secretly inside him. In boyhood he had tried to court her, but she was all for Jack Metheny in those days. Well, Jack was dead now, long dead and moldered away up there on the Little Big Horn with the rest of Custer's command. And Curt Metheny would soon be following after his brother.

Shivering with the intensity of his hatred, Theron Ware kicked a pile of tin cans and bottles into a discordant jangle and strode on, striving to concentrate on the manipulations that would culminate in the death of Curt Metheny. He wouldn't feel right or whole, free and proud and secure again, until Curt was under the ground.

Well, if all went as he anticipated, this would be Curt's last night on earth, and by tomorrow Theron would be a couple of thousand dollars richer.

NINE

In her room at the Mustang Rita Corday was waiting with aching impatience for her man to come. If he were alive and able, he would keep this appointment he had made months ago. He always came when he promised to, and tonight was the night.

This room was her home, her sanctuary, and she sat with the door bolted, not wanting to see or talk to anyone else this night, not even Curt Metheny or old Barnaby. Rose-shaded lamps spread a soft glow on the lace-curtained windows, the satin-draped bed, the leather chairs, and the neat, glittering table and mirror. A faint fragrance filled the room, a perfume as pure and subtle as that of wild flowers.

When the news had come from Arrowhead, Rita had been horribly afraid that Jakes had been killed there. In dreams of late she had seen him dead, and the fear persisted, despite the account in the Holly Town *Herald* that identified the three dead outlaws as men known only as Laredo, Wind River, and Comanche. But eyewitnesses reported that others of the gang had been severely wounded, hanging helpless in their saddles when the raiders fled from the flaming street and town. Jakes might have been one of those hard hit and might by now be dead and buried in a lonely unmarked grave in the wilderness. Rita refused to believe this, but she couldn't altogether deny the possibility.

I've got to get him away from that outfit, she thought in quiet desperation. *Perhaps I can keep him here tonight, not let him go back. It's just a matter of time before they'll all be shot down. But he's so loyal to Utah Tyrrell, I don't know. There's enough money to make a new start somewhere, his and mine saved together. But he'll want to ride it out with Utah and the rest, until they're all clear—or dead. That's the kind of a man he is, and it could get him killed.*

Theron Ware was in the Mustang now; Rita could hear his crisp, deep authoritative voice in the hall. Theron was handsome enough, but tainted with evil. She wondered how a girl like Lenora Forbes could endure Theron—it was rumored that they were to be married. With Theron rising to esteem in the bank, old Hoop Forbes probably figured it was a fine match for his daughter. Rita pitied Lenora from the bottom of her heart.

After an interval of pacing about the room, Rita sat down at the dressing table to brush her red-gold hair with long, rhythmic strokes. She had her mother's lush beauty, but not her singing voice. She wondered how different her life would have been if Selma had lived. *Mama wanted me to be a great actress,* Rita thought, with irony. *And I end up in a place like the Mustang, waiting for an outlaw lover.*

She rose and walked the floor again, the yearning hunger for him like a hollow ache within her. Why didn't he come? How long could a woman stand this kind of a life, never wholly alive except when with him?

Rita knew his footsteps the moment she heard them in the corridor, and she was unbolting the door before he reached it. Inside the room with the door locked behind him, Jakes kissed her and held her for a long time without speaking. When they parted, he sank wearily into a chair with booted legs stretched before him.

She saw how gaunt and tired he looked, worn to the bone, as she poured drinks from a bottle of brandy. His clothes were ragged and dusty, and he wore a bandage on his left wrist, crusted black with blood and dirt. She never noticed the eye patch any more.

"It's nothing," he said, noting her glance at his wrist, but Rita quickly cut off the bandage, cleansed the raw groove a bullet had left, and put on a clean dressing.

"It was bad—up there?" she murmured.

"And ever since," he said. "Bad enough, Rita. But I'm here now."

"Don't go back, darling," she pleaded. "Stay with me and get rested up. You're tired to death. Then we'll go away somewhere, start a new life for ourselves. We've got enough money saved to do it now."

"Not yet. I can't leave Utah and the boys in a fix like that. We've got to pull one more job, Rita. Then we're going to break up."

"It's always the last one that kills you."

Jakes smiled. "If Arrowhead didn't kill us, we ought to live forever. Don't worry, Rita, it won't be long now." He sipped the brandy with grateful appreciation. "This sure tastes good, baby."

"Have you got to buy provisions?" asked Rita.

"I gave Barnaby the list. I think the old man can be trusted."

"Yes, Barney's a good man."

"He works in the bank, too," Jakes said musingly. "Could he be Utah's contact man here?"

"He might be. Barney doesn't think much of the law in Holly Town."

Jakes downed his drink and held out the glass for a refill. "You don't know who leaves those messages here for Utah?" He drank, stretched, and sighed luxuriously in the comfortable chair.

"No, I don't."

"Well, I'll probably meet the man later."

Rita lifted his chin in her hand. "You want a bath, sweetie? I'll get a tub of water."

"No, I washed up in the river." He laughed in quiet delight. "Sweetie! It always gets me when you call me that. Bowie and Herm ought to hear it."

"You are sweet," Rita said with a fond smile.

"Your eyes are shining. Your face is sparkling."

"You always make me sparkle, you know. Are you hungry, darling?"

"For you," Jakes said. "Come here."

Rita went into his arms. "It's been so long, so awful long."

"Pretty soon we'll be together all the time. So much that you'll get sick of seeing me around, most likely."

"Never!" she cried, "You know better than that, sweetie—Oh, here's something you'll like." She handed him the pipe he had left on his last visit, filled with fresh tobacco now, and Jakes lit up with deep pleasure.

"I've missed this old pipe," he said, smiling and blowing fragrant blue smoke at her. "Rita, it's really like coming home."

"I want a home of our own," she whispered into the smoke.

"We'll have one, baby."

"Why—why do you have to go back out there?"

"Because Utah needs me, needs me bad," Jakes said simply. "And he's too good a man to let down, Rita. But it'll be over, early next week. And I'll come after you, or meet you in Lodestone. Or send for you, if it's too hot hereabouts."

Rita lowered her glass. "You going to hit some place in Holly?"

"I don't know for sure—yet. But we've got to

make one more good haul—somewhere. I've got some money cached away, thanks to you. But the rest of the boys are flat, Rita. We figured on quitting after Arrowhead. But all we got there was a lot of lead."

"That must have been terrible."

"It was quite a nightmare," Jakes admitted, eyes narrowing at the memory.

"Did any more die—on the trail?"

"Spanish went under. And I'm afraid Old Pitts is going."

Rita shuddered, drained her glass, then poured two more drinks. Jakes lounged back in relaxed contentment, tasting the brandy and puffing on his pipe. "This is like heaven, Rita. After a long campaign in hell." He accepted the refill and held up his glass. "To us, Rita—and our new life."

They clicked glasses, drank together, and then she was in his arms. She saw him reach out to turn down the lamp, and whispered, "Leave it lighted, darling. I want to see you. I want to see your dear face."

Later, drinking and smoking cigarettes in drowsy, peaceful comfort, Rita could sense his slow withdrawal. "It's going to be harder than ever to leave you, baby," he said, but already, she knew, he was riding back to meet his comrades. Already gone from her a little, back to his world of men and guns and horses. Love might be a woman's whole existence, but it was never more than one part of a man's life. And wakeful now, she could see Jakes dead, as she had seen him in the dreams that tormented her sleeping. *If he goes this time, he'll never come back to me,* she thought with a dreadful certainty. But there was nothing she could do to hold him, and she bit back her impulse to tell him of her fears.

When Rita brought the steak suppers back from the kitchen, Jakes was slightly impatient to be on his way. He said nothing to that effect, but Rita knew what he was feeling, and thinking, behind that black-patched mask of a face. The fine tragic face she loved so much.

Jakes ate with a hearty appetite, cleaning up his plate and then finishing the steak Rita had been picking at without hunger. "I needed that meal, almost as much as I needed you," Jakes said. "At the rate we've been eating it ought to last me a week." After a third cup of coffee he loaded and lighted his pipe and got up to strap on his guns.

"You don't have to go this early," protested Rita, in alarm.

"It's a long ride, and I don't want to be out in too much daylight," Jakes said. "I'd better pull out now, Rita, much as I hate to leave you."

"All right," she said with quiet resignation. "I'll be waiting—as usual."

"Don't be sad, baby. You'll hear from me Saturday or Sunday. If I can't get to you, I'll send word somehow. Tell you where to meet me."

Rita smiled wanly. "It's foolish to say be careful—but please be as careful as you can, my darling."

"I will, Rita, don't you fret. One more job and we're all through."

"We'll have to go a long way out of this Ontawee country, in order to be safe."

"That's all right, isn't it?" said Jakes, smiling cheerfully. "As long as we're together, Rita, it don't matter where we are."

"Oh, my dearest—" She kissed him hard and clung fiercely to him on parting, but she did not weep until he had left the room.

In the darkened kitchen old Barnaby was waiting for Jakes with the money left over from the purchases he'd made. Barney said the packhorse was all loaded and ready to travel, and Jakes told him to keep the change.

"You aren't hooked up with Utah, are you?" inquired Jakes.

"No, but I wouldn't mind being," Barnaby said. "And I got a friend who wants to ride out with you tonight."

"Who's that?"

"Boy by the name of Curt Metheny. One of the best."

Jakes blinked his one eye, the muscles riding along his clean jawbone. "Tell your friend to stay put, Barney. It's no time to join up with us—it's too late. We're busting up as soon as we get in the clear."

"All right, I'll tell him," Barnaby said. "But listen, Jakes—there's a man waiting for you, I think, out in the horse shed. Theron Ware, he works in the bank. Dunno what he wants of you, but I wouldn't put too much trust in him."

Jakes grinned. "I wouldn't trust a banker at all, Barney. But I guess I can handle him. Maybe he's our man here."

"Could be," confessed Barney. "Theron likes to play all four sides against the middle. Well, I'm obliged, Jakes, and good luck to you."

"I'm thanking you, Barney," said Jakes, shaking hands and stepping out the back door, to cross toward the horse shed with long, elastic strides. After a moment Barnaby followed him outside, and angled off through the shadows to where Curt Metheny was waiting for him.

In the blackness of the shed, One-Eyed Jakes spotted Ware's white shirt front and moved toward it, right hand near his gun. "What do you want, mister?"

"Just a few words with you, friend," Theron Ware said coolly.

"Well, let's hear them."

"How'd you like to make some quick, easy money tonight?"

"I haven't got time," Jakes said, studying the banker in the vague dimness.

"You could use some money, couldn't you?" Theron said, suave and superior as he returned the scrutiny.

"Money always comes in handy. What's the proposition?"

"I want a man killed. In fact, the whole town wants this man killed. A hundred dollars in advance; another hundred after the job's done."

"Life's cheap in Holly Town," drawled Jakes. "Who's the man?"

"His name is Curt Metheny," said Theron. "You'll find him at the livery stable. I'll keep the law off you."

One-Eyed Jakes seemed to grow taller and broader, his features bleak as bone, and Theron Ware shrank from him in the deep shadows of the horse shed. "I don't kill that way," Jakes said, with contempt. "Why don't you do it yourself?"

"I have a position and reputation to uphold in this town."

"Ah, yes, the young banker." Jakes's laughter was scornful. "Besides which, you lack the guts to try it."

Theron Ware stood silent, his face expressionless, his eyes flashing darkly.

"Do you have any connection with Utah Tyrrell?" asked Jakes. "A message for him maybe?"

Ignoring the question, Theron Ware spoke at last in cold, clipped tones: "Evidently there's nothing else for us to discuss. But you're passing up some easy money, friend. I could raise the stakes, if necessary."

Jakes eyed him with loathing. "You haven't got enough money in that damn bank to buy my gun."

Theron Ware shrugged his tailored shoulders. "Have it your own way, then."

"If anything happens to Metheny, I'll know who's responsible."

"What's Curt Metheny to you, anyway?"

"He's a friend of Barney's," said Jakes. "That's enough for me. Now you take a walk, mister, and I'll get ready to move out."

Theron Ware shrugged once more, forced a grimace of disdain, and left the shed to saunter across the yard toward the back porch of the Mustang. Jakes watched him go, one eye narrowed to a slit of pale fire, lips thinned tautly on his teeth. "I ought to blast him wide open," he murmured to himself. "But maybe he is Utah's man, even if he wouldn't admit it to me." Jakes turned to untie the horses, attach a rope to his saddle, and lead both animals out of the shed.

Swinging aloft with lithe ease, a high, spare shape against the star-sown sky, Jakes settled himself in the cool leather and started to ride out. Bowie and Herm were going to be surprised to see him back—*if* he got back. That banker had a greedy, bounty-hunting look in his eyes.

Looking on from the shadowed corner of a

nearby woodshed, Curt Metheny and Barnaby saw Theron Ware reach furtively in under his left arm and wheel about in a tense crouch near the Mustang's back steps, bringing his pistol to bear upon the back of One-Eyed Jakes.

Curt Metheny drew and fired with instinctive flowing speed, lining his shot in front of Ware before Theron could press the trigger. Window-glass shattered beyond the banker, and Theron switched his aim to their direction, blazing away at Curt's fading muzzle flash. Curt and Barnaby felt the whiplash passage of bullets, and Barney jerked back, swearing in the middle of his draw, as splinters from the shed wall blinded his eyes and stung his cheeks.

After one fleeting backward glance, One-Eyed Jakes booted his bronc into a gallop, yanking the packhorse along after them, and they vanished behind the moonlit outbuildings of the back area, leaving dust surging and clods of dirt pelting in their wake. The reports echoed away from wall to wall along the row of houses, as doors burst open and shouts rose in the night.

Curt Metheny threw another shot at Ware, holding low in the tricky light and spraying Theron's legs with gravel. Theron's gun blossomed fire again, the slugs chewing wood from the shed at their backs, and old Barnaby got his gun out and let go a couple of quick blasts that clanged and screeched off metal garbage cans on the porch near Ware's white-hatted head. As Curt's Colt hammered once more, Theron broke and ran for it, disappearing round the far corner of the Mustang. Curt and Barney holstered their smoking .44s and ducked off in the opposite direction as more doors slammed open and blurred forms erupted into backyards all along the line.

Well away from the scene, they slowed to a walk, and Barnaby panted: "That money-grubbing bastard! Wanted the reward money himself. A damn banker. Can you tie that one?"

"Nothing about Theron would surprise me, Barney," said Curt. "I should've put that first one right through his skull. I wish to hell I had."

"You'll get another chance at him, Curt," said Barnaby, digging splinters out of his gray whiskers.

"I won't get another chance to join up with Utah Tyrrell. Theron queered that for me."

"Jakes wasn't going to take you anyway, Curt. He told me it was too late. The gang's breaking up right soon—if they don't get caught and strung up first."

"Well, it was just a dream, Barney. The kind that never comes true, I guess." Curt smiled and shook his head. "At least we gave Jakes a little help."

"Theron's a good shot, Curt," said Barnaby. "Jakes would've been a dead man if you hadn't snapped that shot off when you did. You're real fast, son. I used to be myself, and I've seen a lot of good ones, and I *know.* They don't come much faster than you, Curt."

"A helluva lot of good it does me," Curt muttered.

"It'll pay off for you sometime, mark my word."

"Maybe, Barney, maybe," Curt Metheny murmured absently. "Say, there's something familiar looking about that One-Eyed Jakes. I spotted it when I first saw him at the river crossing."

Barnaby nodded. "Yeah, I've noticed that myself, come to think of it. But damned if I can figure out who he puts me in mind of."

"I can't say either. Reminds me some of Dad, I think. The way he moves and sits a horse and carries his head and shoulders. But I don't know—" Curt turned to glance down the line, which was quiet and orderly once more. "We ought to go back and tell Rita that Jakes got away all right, Barney."

"Yeah, we better do that, Curt. The poor gal will be all tore up. A nice fellah, that Jakes. Like some that your dad and me used to ride with. Maybe the last of the real ones, him and Utah. Wish I could think just who he reminds me of now."

"Well, he's gone, Barney," said Curt Metheny. "And we'll never see him again."

TEN

Theron Ware was knocking balls about the pool table in an alcove off the main gaming hall of the Silver Queen. The smooth flight of the gay-colored ivories over the green velvet surface pleased his fancy. He liked the bright shifting patterns that evolved under his cue stick, and the emphatic *sock* of a ball driven clean and hard into a leather pocket. He paused, stood the cue against the wall, and finished eating his thick roast beef sandwich, washing it down with milk. Theron did not drink liquor and seldom smoked, unless offered a cigar by Hooper Forbes or J. A. Cottrell. He was contemptuous of people addicted to the minor vices of drinking and smoking.

Emptying the pockets then, he racked the balls, broke them with delicate finesse, and started shooting with earnest concentration. Reeling off one difficult shot after another, Theron proceeded to clean the table with methodical precision. Too bad he couldn't have been this accurate with his pistol last night, Theron reflected sourly. But moonbeams and shadows had made the light deceptive, and the range had been long for handguns. Curt and Barney hadn't scored any more than Theron.

He was alone in the poolroom at this forenoon hour, and the bar and gambling hall were deserted except for the swampers at their cleaning chores. Theron Ware was waiting for someone he had summoned to meet him under cover, but waiting without impatience. It was a relief to escape from the bank, and J. A. had accepted his fabricated excuse without comment or question.

Yes, I had my chance at Curt Metheny last night, Theron thought, slamming the black eight-ball savagely into a corner pocket. *And I missed him.* But Theron realized that perhaps it was just as well he hadn't shot Curt, since J. A. Cottrell disapproved of shooting under any circumstances. Still, it irked Theron immensely that Curt had spoiled his chance of collecting a couple of thousand dollars in reward money. It would be better, however, to have somebody else take care of Curt. As soon as Alvah Parkhurst showed up, Metheny's hours would be numbered.

The ornate batwing doors squealed on their hinges, and Theron looked out through the casino and saw the swaggering hulk of the young man he was expecting. Parkhurst's clothing was worn and soiled, but his brass-studded belt and holster gleamed from polished care. He had an ugly, sullen look that Theron found promising, but he didn't appear to be very bright or smart. Under a weather-stained hat, overlong hair hung raggedly about Parkhurst's coarse features, and a heavy chin jutted beneath his sulky mouth. An ignorant and obnoxious lout, Theron decided. But that made no difference as long as he did the job.

Parkhurst strutted into the poolroom and stood with grimy fists on hips, watching Ware rack the balls once more.

"You want to see me, mister?" There was nothing humble, or even respectful, in Parkhurst's tone and manner.

"Want to shoot a game?" Theron glanced at the outer room and observed no one there who counted. "Kill a little time. We can talk as we play."

"I ain't much good at pool," Parkhurst said, with the obvious inference that the game was far beneath the interest of a gun fighter.

"Pick out a stick," Theron Ware said, with amused tolerance. "I'll break 'em up good for you." He called a bank shot on the corner ball and scattered them all over the table, but the ball didn't quite drop.

Awkward and ill at ease with the cue, Alvah Parkhurst missed the easy setup and laughed as if he hadn't really tried to sink it.

"Understand you're pretty good with a gun," Theron said, bending over the table and cutting the red three into a side pocket.

"Good enough to get by, I guess."

"Think you could take Curt Metheny?"

Parkhurst's thick features lighted up. "You're damn right! And I'm going to some of these days."

"Why not today, Al?" asked Theron Ware. "There are many prominent citizens who'd like to get rid of Metheny. He's a public nuisance, a troublemaker, and a menace to the community. They were going to hire a gunman from outside, but I advocated utilizing local talent. I thought you might want the job."

A bit bewildered by the flow of fancy language, Alvah Parkhurst scratched his stubbled jaw. "How much they paying?"

"One hundred dollars."

That was obviously a lot of money to Parkhurst, but he shrewdly sensed the possibility of getting more. "That ain't enough."

"A hundred in advance then," Theron said. "A hundred more after you finish the job." He missed his shot, leaving another easy setup.

"That's better." Parkhurst punched the ball into the corner pocket. "But it still ain't much for gunning a man like Curt Metheny."

"Do you want it or not?" Theron demanded, with an abrupt change of tactics, tired of toying with this oaf.

"I'll take it," Parkhurst said. "I was going to get Curt, anyway. What've I got to lose?"

"Nothing but your life," Theron Ware said, racking his cue. "Come on in the back room and have a drink."

"Let me worry about my life, mister," said Alvah Parkhurst, following Theron into a small, secluded room, where a bottle and glass waited on the table. Alvah reached for the bottle, then looked questioningly at Ware.

"Go ahead, help yourself," Theron said. "But you'd better not drink too much today. Or do any talking at all about this."

"Don't fret, brother," laughed Parkhurst, swallowing a glassful of the whiskey. "I can handle liquor like I handle a gun. But what about Marshal Gracey?"

"If you take Curt in a fair fight, it'll be self-defense. The law won't bother you. If you have to take him some other way, we'll still get you off. Don't worry on that score. Just make sure you get him."

"I'll get him, all right." Parkhurst threw down another drink and grinned with cocksure confidence. "Curt won't live to see sundown."

Theron Ware handed him a thin sheaf of crisp bills. "Here's a hundred. You'll get the rest when Metheny's dead."

Parkhurst thumbed through the bank notes. "I don't want to go to jail for this, mister."

"You won't. All the big men in town are behind you, Al. And public opinion is one hundred per cent against Curt Metheny."

"Where will I find him?" Parkhurst was still counting the money, with evident pleasure.

"In the livery barn—or around town," Theron said. "That's your job now."

"Consider it done, brother." Alvah Parkhurst tossed off his third slug, set down the glass, and corked the bottle. He glanced at Ware, expecting a handshake to seal the bargain, but Theron was inspecting his gold watch. Parkhurst shrugged and said "See you later" as he swaggered out the door.

Theron Ware remained alone in that back room for several minutes. He felt none of the satisfaction and triumph he had anticipated. For one of the few times in his life, he was sick with shame and self-loathing. He tried to shake it off, but the feeling clung like a second layer of skin, scurvy and ulcerous. Suddenly he saw himself exposed in the glaring light of truth and reality; it was not a pleasant sight.

Theron, like many of the other people of Holly Town, knew Alvah Parkhurst's story. Alvah had been living with his mother, who was separated from Zed Parkhurst, when it happened. At the time neither mother nor son had grieved much, for Zed was no longer involved in their lives. But now that Alvah wanted to make his mark as a gunman, he had adopted the motive of revenge. It made a good yarn in the saloons: a bereaved boy out to avenge the killing of his father. Alvah Parkhurst had been in some shooting matches here and there, and had wounded a few opponents. He was quick and accurate with a pistol, from long intensive practice, and after downing Metheny he'd be on his way to fame and fortune. A gun fighter could still command top wages on the frontier. Two hundred dollars for this day's work. A good cowhand had to work half a year for that much cash, along with his board and keep.

Parkhurst had told and retold his mission-of-revenge tale many times, and such, Theron Ware knew, was his mentality that he'd come to believe it himself.

Slow and fumbling, unfit to hold his head up, Theron let himself out a rear door of the Silver Queen and walked back toward the bank like a man in a deep trance.

Toward evening, while alone in the livery stable, Curt Metheny heard the tinkle of oversized spurs and turned and wallowed through hay to the edge of the loft. He was aware of some danger before he saw the man in the runway below. It must be young Parkhurst; Dane and Tee Dee had told him that Alvah was in town. Curt felt a familiar chill prickle up his spine and tighten his scalp. He could see that this hulking kid was all worked up, keyed for violent action, with hatred plain in his eyes and face. And Curt's gunbelt was hanging from a peg on a roughhewn upright fifteen feet away. Pitchfork in hand, Curt waited, calm on the outside, quivering cold within.

"I'm going to kill you, Metheny," said the man, elbows wide and right hand clawed as he glared upward.

"Who the hell are you, anyway?" Curt asked.

"I'm Alvah Parkhurst."

"I don't even know you."

"But I know you, all right. Your old man killed my father."

Curt smiled, feeling the sweat bead his face and drip from his armpits as he sidled toward his gunbelt. "What's that got to do with us? They tell me you didn't even know your father. And mine paid for whatever he did."

"You can't weasel outa this, Metheny," said Parkhurst, lips skinned back on horselike teeth. "Save your breath."

"This don't make any sense at all, boy."

"It does to me, Metheny. And I'm calling the turn here."

"Who's paying you, Park?" asked Curt, forcing another smile.

Parkhurst's laugh sounded hoarse and strained. "Nobody has to pay me for this. It's purely a pleasure."

"I haven't got a gun on me." Curt was still inching toward that upright beam, sweat glistening on his brown face and soaking his shirt.

"That's too bad," jeered Parkhurst. "The way I hear it, my father didn't have one neither when your old man murdered him—and your mother." Alvah Parkhurst was on the brink of drawing, and Curt's .44 was still far beyond reach.

"Can't we talk this over, Park?" drawled Curt,

stalling for time. Dane and the others ought to be back from supper, or somebody else might come in and break this up. If they didn't come soon, Curt Metheny was done for. His right hand shifted and tightened on the smooth haft of the fork, and sweat stung like acid in his slitted green eyes.

"Not by a damn sight!" Parkhurst gritted out. "I'm going to put the first one right in your guts, Metheny."

"You'll hang for it, boy."

"Oh no, I won't!" Parkhurst laughed in mockery. "I'll probably get a medal for it. Everybody in Holly wants you dead, Metheny. When you're dead, I'll plant your gun in your hand. Self-defense, Metheny, and I'll be a big hero in this town."

"You'll never get away with it," Curt told him. "Theron Ware'll turn you over to the law, you fool."

"You're a dead man, Metheny!"

"And you're a brave man," Curt said. "Shooting an unarmed man out of a hayloft. It sure takes a lot of nerve, Park."

"Go after your gun, damn your stinking hide!" Parkhurst bellowed. "I see it hanging up there. Go for it, damn you!"

Metheny gestured with his left arm, and secured a tight throwing grip on the fork handle with his right hand. "I wouldn't get halfway to it, Park."

"Die where you are then!" snarled Alvah Parkhurst, right arm whipping into his draw, and raising his .45 to fire upward. The flame streaked wickedly in the yellow lamplight, the report booming loud in the vast barn.

Curt Metheny, dodging as the man drew, felt the searing breath of the slug as he poised the pitchfork high over his right shoulder. Alvah was lining his pistol again when Curt flung the fork down at him with free-armed power and speed, tines first, the thin steel shimmering in the shadowy light. Parkhurst sidestepped, his gun jerking and blaring up at the rafters, but one tine stabbed deep into his left shoulder, the impact jarring him back against the door of a box stall. Alvah bounced off the wood and reeled forward, the long-handled fork jutting in front of him.

Stalled horses were bucking and plunging, kicking and bugling in panic, and a slow, murky rain of dust and hay chaff trickled from the ceiling, as Curt Metheny took off from the wooden ledge in a reckless flying leap. Parkhurst's gun exploded into the floor, lifting gouts of earth and straw as Curt's driving boots struck Alvah in the chest and smashed him back on the stall door. Alvah screamed at the cruel wrench of steel in his shoulder, and the pistol fell slithering out of his loosened grasp.

Curt toppled backward from the jolting collision, and both men went down rolling and scrambling about on the dirt floor, stunned and breathless. When they came upright at last, panting and weaving, Parkhurst yanked the fork free from his bloody shoulder to reverse the tines and charge like a wounded maniac, thrusting and stabbing viciously at Metheny.

Retreating before the flashing steel points, Curt dodged and feinted and watched for an opening, his arms raked and slashed before he could lunge in and grab the handle just behind the tines. Then, jerking Alvah forward with his right hand on the fork, Curt hooked his left fist savagely into Alvah's face, striking swiftly again and again.

Parkhurst's heavy features crimsoned under the lashing left hand, his head rocking far back on his bull neck, and Curt ripped the hayfork loose and threw it aside. Alvah tried to fight back one-handed, his left arm dangling numb and useless from the blood-drenched shoulder, but Curt Metheny kept circling to Parkhurst's left, crossing his right fist over that limp arm with hammer-like force and precision, shaking and staggering the big man with every solid punch.

Shag-head bobbing and snapping, Parkhurst lurched back against the box stall and sagged there, a bleeding hulk. Aflame with fighting fury and hitting Alvah with both hands now, Curt Metheny went on beating that shapeless scarlet face, flogging the large head against the wooden door, until Parkhurst crumpled in complete collapse and slid slack and senseless on his back in the straw and dirt and horse manure.

For a moment Curt stood over him too weary to move, sobbing for breath and swaying on his feet, with raw-knuckled fists hanging at his sides. Then, with a heaving effort, he turned and stumbled out through the archway, to lave his sore hands and arms and bury his head and face in the water trough. When he straightened from the tub, cooled and dripping and somewhat restored, a man was sitting there on a buckboard wagon, watching Curt in curious wonder.

"What's going on here?" the man inquired.

"There's a boy hurt inside," Curt said, hoarse and labored. "Will you give me a hand—and take him to the doctor?"

"Sure will, son." The driver got down and trailed Curt into the barn, halting in stricken amazement at the sight of Parkhurst. "Suffering Gawd!" he said, in awed tones, staring down at the blood-smeared unconscious bulk. "He's beat to death, ain't he?"

"Not quite," Curt Metheny said. "He came in here to shoot me—I don't know why. Didn't have a gun on me."

The man eyed the red-tipped pitchfork, wagged his head, and stopped to help Curt lift the heavy body. Between them they carried Parkhurst outside, dumped him in the wagon bed, and the man climbed aboard to drive away toward Doc Pillon's house.

The yard and barn were filling up with excited men who had heard the gunshots, as Curt went back inside to pick up Parkhurst's .45, and then climb the ladder to the hayloft, where he buckled on his own gunbelt. When Curt descended the ladder, an eager crowd swarmed about him, jabbering questions and theories as to what had occurred.

Curt Metheny attempted to explain, saw disbelief grow on the faces clustered around him, and finally said, "Oh, to hell with it. You all got your own ideas, I guess." Shouldering his way roughly through the ranked men, he strode off toward his room at the rear of the stable.

He was swabbing his cut arms and swollen knuckles with a wet towel when Dane Lauritsen and little Tee Dee came in to settle down alongside of him, their faces drawn with anxiety.

"What happened, Curt?" asked Lauritsen. "Why didn't you tell those men about it?"

"What's the use?" Curt sighed wearily, and drank from a pint bottle of whiskey. "I tried to tell 'em, but nobody believed me. I could see it in their faces."

"I believe you, Curt!" cried Tee Dee. "I know you always tell things straight and honest."

"I believe you, too," Lauritsen said. "Young Parkhurst's been threatening to get you for a

137

long time now. Looks like he finally got around to it."

"He tried," Curt said, and described briefly for them just how it had been.

Dane Lauritsen nodded solemnly. "I'll back you, Curt. They can't pin any blame on you in this case."

"But they will, Dane. You know damn well they will."

"I won't stand for it," Lauritsen declared. "I won't let them."

Curt Metheny smiled at them, sweat starting out anew on his lean face and glittering in his cropped sandy hair. "Glad I got you two—and old Barney. To hell with the rest of 'em—But it sure beats me how they won't let me alone. A gun-happy kid I don't even know, coming in here to kill me. Probably someone sent him. Theron Ware maybe—or old Hoop Forbes."

Spurs clinked outside, and Stan Russett came to a rigid stand in the doorway, tall, rugged, and stone-faced. "Come on with me, Curt. You're under arrest."

"What the hell for?" Curt came erect in one fluid motion, and stood facing the deputy, green eyes flaring with cold fire.

"You pitchforked Parkhurst and damn near beat him to death," Russett said. "I guess that's enough. Don't give me any trouble."

"He came here to shoot me," Curt Metheny

138

said. "I didn't have my gun on, so I used what I had. Get the hell out of here, Stan!"

"I'm taking you in, Curt," said Russett steadily.

"You'll have to use that gun," Curt told him. "You want to reach for it?"

Dane Lauritsen rose with lank dignity and moved between them, his back to Curt, his eyes on Russett. "You're after the wrong man, Stan," he said gravely. "Go and arrest Parkhurst. He started all this."

"We'll see, Dane," muttered Russett. "I'll leave Metheny in your custody—for now. Don't let him run off anywhere." The deputy wheeled stiffly away to return to the front of the barn.

Curt took another swig of whiskey and listened to the angry ominous rumble of sound from the massed men at the stable entrance. Lauritsen and Tee Dee were listening too, their faces solemn and worried.

"Wish I had that shotgun," Dane Lauritsen murmured, shifting nervously in the rawhide chair.

"Here's my Winchester, Dane," said Curt, handing over the rifle, which Lauritsen laid across his bony knees.

Tee Dee got up from the bunk and paused at the door. "I'll see what's going on out there."

Curt Metheny rose and paced the room, the tanned skin stretched taut over the high bones of his face. "If they try to take me, some of them will die."

"I'll stand with you on that, Curt," promised Dane Lauritsen.

When Tee Dee returned, Barnaby was stumping along behind him, a sawed-off shotgun in the crook of his arm.

"Ed Gracey come and took charge and bawled the living daylights outa Stan Russett," announced Tee Dee with gleeful satisfaction. "Dressed Stan down for fair and sent him back to the office with his head hanging low. Ed says he's going to arrest Alvah Parkhurst and find out who hired him to go after you, Curt."

Barnaby nodded his gray head in confirmation. "Ed's still a tough old rooster. He put a stop to the lynching talk, and he'll have that mob broke up in a few minutes' time. You're clear as can be, Curt."

"With the law maybe," Curt Metheny conceded, grinning ruefully. "But not so far as Holly Town's concerned. They won't let me off that easy, Barney."

And Curt was right. The story grew and spread around Holly and throughout the Ontawee, and Curt Metheny was the villain. He had used a pitchfork on that poor, half-witted Parkhurst punk, and then beaten the boy almost to death with his fists. Ed Gracey, on behalf of the law, had cleared Metheny, but something ought to be done about Curt. It was like having a mad dog in the community. The mob had dispersed, but the lynch talk continued. Curt ought to be strung up, like his father before him. If Curt wasn't done away with, he'd go on a rampage someday and kill even more men than his father had killed.

Ed Gracey had found ninety-odd dollars on Alvah Parkhurst, most of it in crisp new bills, which was ample evidence that someone had paid Alvah to go gunning for Metheny. "How else would that stupid ox get hold of a hundred bucks?" Ed Gracey remarked. But even this disclosure failed to change public opinion and aid Curt's cause in any way.

In the town that night and all day Friday, Curt was more than ever a renegade outcast, hemmed in on all sides by hostility and hatred. On the street women turned their backs to him, and men spat and shook their fists at him as he passed by. Some restaurants and saloons refused to serve him, and Curt resorted to eating in his room, sending Tee Dee out to the Greek's after food and drink.

ELEVEN

On Saturday night, Curt Metheny was a little drunk when he left the Ten-High Saloon, one place in town that would still serve him, but he carried it so well it was scarcely discernible, except in the intensity of his green eyes.

But Curt knew he was a bit overboard, and he had an idea that everyone else knew it. He had come to feel that his drinking was obvious and much discussed, that people were forever watching, condemning and talking about him. Since the brawl with Parkhurst, Curt felt it even more.

"Curt Metheny's got a load on, he's cockeyed drunk again," he fancied folks were saying. *"A chip off the old block, a drunkard like his old man—and dangerous, too. Apt to go on a killing spree any time. . . . Well, what can you expect? It's in his blood."*

It was a bad night to be drunk, with all of Frying Pan in town for the dance, and Stan Russett still looking for a chance to lock Curt up. Alvah Parkhurst was still bedded down at Doc Pillon's, and under arrest for assault with intent to kill, but there might be other hired gunhands hunting for Metheny.

Curt had been too full of pent-up bitterness and emotion to refrain from drinking tonight, and too defiant to remain in seclusion. But he wouldn't get too drunk to handle a gun, or his fists. Fully aware of the danger, he was determined to walk the streets of Holly this Saturday night, as free and easy as any other inhabitant of the town. His knuckles were still raw and sore from the beating he had given Parkhurst, and his forearms still burned from those pitchfork gashes. But he was fit and ready for any kind of action.

He paused to shape and light a cigarette, by the scarred post of a boarded overhang, aware that passing people slanted furtive glances at him, and then looked quickly away. The old fury and hatred flamed higher than ever in him. He hated this town and almost everybody in it. He wished his brother Jack were alive; together they could have treed this town. But Curt was alone, and the odds were high.

He wanted more to drink, but his money was gone. Dane Lauritsen had withheld most of his pay this week. "For your own good, Curt," Dane had said. "You're in a mood to cut loose and get yourself into real serious trouble. I don't want that to happen to you, son—" So Curt would have to borrow a few dollars in order to do any more drinking.

Stan Russett passed him in silence, giving Curt a cold, close scrutiny, and Curt stared straight back at the deputy, his bruised hands knotting into fists. *You'll be one of the first to get it,*

Stanko, thought Metheny. *That tin badge won't save you when the time comes.*

Farther along Curt saw Theron Ware talking importantly with J. A. Cottrell, Hooper Forbes, and other prosperous businessmen and ranchers, all of whom pointedly ignored Curt's passing. On the outer fringe of the group was Pat Shannon, the boyhood friend who had become a freighter, and Pat also failed to recognize Curt. It cut and rankled, but it was Theron Ware that Curt felt the most hatred for. *You'll get it early too, Theron. You'll never live to marry Lenora Forbes.*

At the corner of Front and River Streets, Curt halted and leaned against an empty hitch rail before the solid gray bulk of the adobe-block building. A light glimmered faintly inside, where old Barnaby was completing his duties as caretaker. The bank that had foreclosed on Judson Metheny's livery stable, and later on his saddle and harness shop. The bank that held the fortunes of Hooper Forbes and all the other big augers. The bank that Curt wanted to hold up and rob—

He wished he could lead Utah Tyrrell's bunch in to take the place, break the bank, ruin the town and the spreads outside, and then shoot their way out, leaving the dead strewn along the street. That would settle Curt Metheny's score against this community and its people in one savage stroke. But it was a dream, as remote as the stars beyond the distant ramparts of the Rockies.

The lamp blinked out inside the adobe walls, and Barnaby emerged from the building, bent and gnarled and hickory-tough, his sunken eyes and seamed face lighting up as he saw Curt waiting there.

"Glad to see you, son—and sober," he said. "Though you're packing a pretty high-calibered breath for so early in the evening."

"Dane held back most of my wages, Barney."

"Probably a smart thing to do," Barnaby said. "I can spare a few dollars, Curt. But I don't want you getting drunk this Saturday night."

Curt Metheny laughed quietly. "Barney, I don't think there's enough whiskey in the Ontawee to get me drunk tonight."

Barnaby snorted softly. "I useta get that notion myself—but I was most generally wrong. If a man keeps on drinking long enough, he's bound to get drunk. Curt, I understand Ed Gracey can't pry outa Alvah Parkhurst where that hundred came from."

"Theron Ware," said Curt. "It figures that way, Barney."

"But he ain't alone. Theron's got backing in high places. And if they'd pay Parkhurst, they'll pay somebody else to get the job done."

"Let 'em come, Barney." Curt's voice was dull and flat. "Might as well be now as later. And this time it'll be for keeps."

Barnaby sighed and handed him five silver dollars. "Stay sober anyway, son. And keep away from that dance. I know you can hold your liquor, just like Jud did, but it don't help a man much in a showdown. If you've got to drink, Curt, take a bottle to your room."

"That's just what I'm going to do," Curt said. "Thanks a lot, Barney. If you need this five before I get around to paying you, get it off Dane."

"I won't need it," Barnaby said, with a careless gesture. "I'm going to drift round and see what I can find out. Rita Corday got some kinda message from Jakes, and I think Rita's getting ready to move out. Well, maybe I can learn something. A deaf man who reads lips can pick up more news than anybody with good hearing."

Curt Metheny saluted and walked back toward the lights of the business center. At the Ten-High, he hesitated outside the batwings when he saw Lyme Vector, Harry Keech, Doyle Guinness, and other Frying Pan riders lined up at the long bar. There were other saloons, and Curt was still welcome in a few of them. Why walk into trouble here? But this was his favorite barroom, and Frying Pan wasn't going to keep him out of it. To hell with them. If they wanted to force the issue, let it start right here and now.

He split the swing-doors and walked quietly through the smoke-haze to an open space at the bar. His presence was felt instantly. Without speaking or looking at him, men made room for

146

him at the bar, and Frying Pan began to heckle him at once.

"You smell something like horse droppings in here?" inquired Lyme Vector, crinkling his arched beak of a nose.

Doyle Guinness sniffed the air. "That livery-barn smell, you mean? It does seem kinda strong, all of a sudden. Somebody let a horse in this saloon?"

"Naw, Doyle, it's that old pitchfork slinger himself," laughed Harry Keech. "How many men you suppose he's pitchforked today?"

"I dunno, Harry," drawled Lyme Vector. "But they claim he's pure hell fire with that hayfork. Keeps them tines honed up razor sharp. It makes a real mean weapon."

"Yeah, and a man gits strong, working a shovel all day behind them horses," Harry Keech declared. "He not only gits strong, but he *smells* strong!"

"Well, it's a honest, down-to-earth smell," Doyle Guinness said, spitting tobacco juice through his stained gray mustache. "Bartender, give that pitchfork man a drink on me."

"Saturday night, and he's still sober enough to walk on his hind legs," Lyme Vector said, wagging his bird-of-prey head. "I'll buy him one, too. He must be short of money to be so damn sober at this hour."

The bartender, bottle and glass poised, looked

questioningly at Metheny before pouring. Curt, striving to curb a floodtide of temper, shook his head. "No thanks, Greg. I'll buy my own drinks."

"That's a downright insult," Lyme Vector said. "A man refusing to drink your whiskey. No man refuses to drink with me."

"Consider yourself insulted then," Curt told him, and the men standing between them began to move away.

"Let it go, Lyme," said Doyle Guinness, a restraining hand on Vector's taut-muscled arm. "Hoop don't want us in any ruckus tonight."

"All right, Doyle," agreed Lyme Vector, with a shrug of his great shoulders. "I reckon a stableboy can't insult you nohow."

Gregory, the barman, was still awaiting Curt Metheny's order with some impatience. Curt decided to buy a quart and get out of there. Greg started to reach for it, then hesitated deliberately, waiting to see Curt's money. Curt slapped silver on the wood with ringing emphasis, and Gregory nodded and brought up a quart bottle. Lyme Vector burst into jeering laughter, and Curt Metheny turned on him then.

"Something funny, Lyme?"

"Just you, boy," said Vector. "Your credit ain't none too good, is it?"

That did it. Curt stepped toward Vector, and Lyme swung his right hand, slashing the glassful of whiskey into Curt's face. Blinded by the stinging liquid, Curt faltered and wiped at his eyes, and Vector looped a long left to the jaw, twisting Curt's neck and driving him back onto the bar. Before he could recover, Lyme was on top of him, ripping both hands to the head and lifting a brutal knee into Metheny's groin. Torn with agony, Curt drove his right elbow wickedly into the man's throat, and Vector fell back gasping and choking, his Adam's apple convulsed.

Bent double, Curt lunged forward and rammed his shoulder into Lyme's belly, carrying him backward across a table, from which the occupants scattered wildly. Bottles and glasses crashed to the floor; the table collapsed into splintering wreckage; and Curt landed on top of Vector in the debris. As they thrashed about in the sawdust, Lyme reached up to gouge at the eyes, and Curt fastened his fingers on Lyme's neck with a steel grip, digging deep.

Harry Keech started to surge forward, bottle in hand and eyes on Metheny's head, but Doyle Guinness blocked the way and shouldered Harry back. "Let 'em go, just the two of 'em," he ordered. Gregory had laid a sawed-off shotgun across the bar, its twin muzzles gaping at the Frying Pan crew, and across the room old Barnaby was watching narrowly, his withered right hand like a claw near his low-slung .44.

With an explosive upheaval and a lash of long

legs, Lyme Vector finally hurled Curt on overhead, and both men rolled and scrabbled about trying to rise from the littered floor. Sweat varnished their cheeks and plastered the shirts to their bodies as they circled and faked, crouching and wary. Vector was taller and heavier with a longer reach, but Metheny was quicker and smoother, with enough fire and speed to offset his lack of size.

They closed, swinging with unleashed ferocity. Curt took some jarring smashes to the face and head before he could slip inside those tremendous arms. The pattern of their boyhood fight was being repeated here. Stabbing and slashing at close range, Curt beat Vector backward against the bar. Lyme bounced forward off the wood, straining to grapple and crush his slighter opponent, but Curt's hands were lightning-fast, rocking Vector's head, jolting him back on his heels. Once more the bar caught Lyme's shoulders and kept him from going down.

This time when Lyme Vector came off the counter with a buck-toothed snarl, his right hand went flashing toward his gun. Curt, his own .44 sprung from its sheath and lost somewhere on the floor, strode in and struck with shattering force, left and right, feeling the beaked nose and beaver teeth give under his knuckles, the shock of the impacts rippling up his arms.

Vector stiffened up even taller, his Colt

spinning loose in a bright arc through the smoky lamplight, blood gushing from his nose and mouth. Lyme should have dropped then, but instead he heaved himself forward, clawing and clutching Curt to him in a grizzly-bear embrace. Locked tight together, they reeled and whirled about the crowded room, upsetting chairs and tables and scattering spectators as Curt tried to fight his way loose. But Lyme hung on like a long-limbed leech.

It was a mad, primitive combat, each man striving to destroy the other, with fists and elbows, knees and boots. Their tortured faces no longer looked human, and their blood-soaked shirts were shredded to tatters. They bounced off the wall and toppled to the floor with a thud that shook the building. Curt was on the bottom this time, the air crushed from his lungs, but the force of the fall loosened Lyme's hold and Curt bucked and wrenched out from under him, to roll free in the sawdust.

When Curt reached his knees, Lyme Vector was rearing up from all fours to lunge for him, broken-beaked face a hideous mask of crimson. Summoning up strength from deep within him, striking from his kneeling position, Curt Metheny chopped and clubbed at that ruined face, until Vector pitched abruptly sidewise and rolled over to sprawl motionless, flat on his back.

Curt clambered slowly upright on weak,

quivering legs, half-blind with blood and sweat, his lungs pumping fire, his heart bursting against his ribs. Someone thrust his gun at him, and Curt shook off the sawdust before easing it into the leather. Gregory had the shotgun cradled in his elbow, the barrels lined on the Frying Pan men. Curt stumbled to the bar, took his bottle of whiskey, and turned toward the batwings, unaware of all the eyes fixed on him with awe and wonder. As far as men could recall, nobody had ever whipped Lyme Vector before in a barehanded brawl.

Lyme was struggling to get up now, pausing to rest on hands and knees, his shoulders heaving under the torn shirt and blood dripping steadily from his mutilated face. Harry Keech kicked Lyme's pistol along the planks toward him, and Vector grasped it in his huge right hand, bruised eyes flickering with insane hatred at the slender figure of Curt Metheny.

Vector started to lift the gun in the direction of Curt's back, but old Barnaby stepped in and stomped viciously down on that gunhand, grinding the wrist into the floorboards. The Colt fell from Lyme's grip, and he slumped groaning on his face. Holding his own .44 on Keech and his companions, Barney backed away after Curt, while Gregory cocked his shotgun to halt the vengeful Frying Pan rush before it got under-way.

Curt Metheny had swung back alongside of Barnaby, his Colt lined at Keech and Guinness and the rest of the Forbes riders. "Try it, Harry," invited Curt, with cold, intense fury. "Start reaching, Doyle. There's enough of you."

"Go on, Curt, get out of here," Gregory ordered. "The war's over."

The doors swung shut after Curt and Barnaby, and as the two men walked toward the livery stable, Barney said, "You done a good job on Lyme, Curt. Remember that time I pulled him off you, when you was kids? Well, you got him good tonight."

"He's still alive," Curt mumbled, spitting out a mouthful of blood. "I've still got him to kill, Barney—along with some others."

As they entered the barn, Dane Lauritsen, a dead cigar jutting from his yellowish mustache, looked out through the dusty glass wall of the office and shook his balding head.

"So you've been at it again, Curt," he said heavily, coming to the doorway. "I guess there's no use hoping you'll ever change."

"I couldn't help it, Dane," said Curt wearily. "Lyme Vector threw whiskey in my face. Am I supposed to swallow that?"

"I don't know, Curt, I don't know. It looks like you'll just have to get out of town. Before they kill you—or you have to kill some of them."

Barnaby spoke up: "It wasn't Curt's fault, Dane.

I saw the whole thing. Frying Pan forced it on him."

"It's never his fault, but it always happens." Lauritsen turned back to his desk, shaking his narrow head and chewing unhappily on the unlighted cigar.

In his back room, with Tee Dee in attendance and Barnaby on watch at the door, Curt stripped and bathed and dressed in fresh clothing from the skin out, nipping at the bottle now and then. He put on a clean white shirt, his best store suit, and the fine boots that Tee Dee kept polished with loving care. Watching Curt knot a silk scarf at his throat and brush his damp cropped hair, little Tee Dee said fearfully:

"Curt, you ain't going to that dance? You can't go! They'll gang up on you for sure, Curt."

"I hope so, Tee Dee," said Curt, with solemn grimness. "I sure hope they do."

"But you can't take on the whole pack, Curt," protested Tee Dee, his cherubic features fretted with worriment. "You're good, Curt, but you ain't *that* good."

"It's got to come, Tee Dee. And I'm sick and tired of waiting for it, kid."

Leaning on the doorframe, Barnaby frowned at them. "Honest, Curt, I wouldn't go if I was you. Why don't you set down and rest, drink and talk a little here with us. You been through enough for one night."

Curt smiled gravely at him. "I feel pretty good

after that bath. Lyme didn't hurt me much, anyway, Barney."

"I don't like it, boy." Barnaby shook his silvery head. "The odds are way too long. And I'm too damn old to be of any help to you."

"Barney, I don't want you mixing in it," Curt said gently. "You did enough for me when you tromped on Lyme's gun hand."

Barnaby scowled and shifted his chew to the other cheek. "You ain't going to listen to reason, I reckon. Right or wrong, you're set—just like Jud was."

"But I'm not as wrong as he was, Barney—or as they made him look," Curt Metheny murmured, pouring whiskey into two tin cups. "Have a drink with me. I don't think they'll come in here after me."

Barnaby accepted the cup and lowered himself into the rawhide chair. "I wisht I was twenty years younger, Curt—or even ten." He peered at Curt's skinned and swollen knuckles. "Your hands ain't in very good shape, son."

"They're all right, Barney," said Curt, flexing his fingers. "I won't have to use them again tonight, anyway."

Tee Dee said, "You will, Curt, if you go anywheres near that town hall. They'll be laying for you, sure as can be. You ought to stay away from that shindig. What fun is dancing, anyway? It looks awful foolish to me."

Curt laughed and rumpled the boy's curly hair. "I'm just going to the dance because I've got to see Lenora Forbes—for a minute or two. They won't start anything in a public place like that."

"Maybe you're right, Curt," muttered Barnaby. "But I wouldn't want to bet on it."

TWELVE

The Town Hall was bright and gay with lights and music as Curt Metheny approached it, feeling cool and clean but over-dressed and uncomfortable in his best clothes. Lyme had left lumps on Curt's jaws and welts on his cheekbones, but he wasn't cut up or marked too bad. Compared to Vector, Curt had got off real easy.

Men were gathered in laughing groups about the building, from the water trough in the front area to the carriage sheds at the rear, but a chilling silence spread at Curt's appearance, and the glances that flicked his way were dark and cold with hostile resentment. The story of his fight with Lyme Vector had circulated, and observers estimated that Curt's presence here meant more trouble and violence. No one spoke in greeting; men he had known all his life turned their backs on him.

At the front steps Curt hesitated momentarily, on the verge of turning back. He was crazy to come here, but he wanted to see Lenora Forbes. He had decided to leave Holly tomorrow, and he had to say good-by—He went on to pay his fare, hang his gunbelt and hat on a peg in the corridor, and enter the hall. Heads swiveled and voices hummed at his entrance.

Straight and slim, with an easy grace of movement, his bronze head bright in the lamplight,

Curt walked in and surveyed the scene with outward calmness. From his appearance and manner, no one would have suspected the lonely desolation that ached inside him.

The orchestra was playing a waltz, and Lenora was dancing with Theron Ware. Smooth and skillful on the polished floor, they made a striking couple, but neither looked particularly happy tonight. Theron was talking and smiling with all his charm, but the girl in his arms was unresponsive. Before the number ended, Theron himself went silent and sullen. He escorted Lenora to her chair on the opposite side of the hall, then left her with a stiff nod and disappeared into the milling crowd.

The next set was a quadrille, which Lenora danced with a red-faced young rancher from the Little Ontawee, and Theron Ware had not returned when that figure was finished. As the musicians swung into another waltz tune, Curt crossed the hardwood and stood before Lenora who looked up at him in wide-eyed surprise and a trace of alarm.

"Curt! I didn't expect to see you here."

He laughed shortly. "Nobody did, I guess."

"Sit down, please." She indicated the empty chair at her side.

"Don't you want to dance, Lenny?"

"I'm tired, Curt. And it would only cause trouble."

"Everything I do seems to cause trouble." Curt sighed and sat down next to her, painfully aware that people were staring. "Can't you get out of here, Len?"

Lenora shook her head. "No, no, Curt. I'd like to, but—Oh, it's no use. Why don't you leave, Curt? Before he comes back."

"We could meet somewhere outside."

"Don't you suppose I've thought about that?" she murmured. "But it would never do—the way things are."

"Why not, Lenny?" asked Curt urgently. "We've got something—something real and big and beautiful. Or we could have. Haven't we wasted enough time?"

"Please, Curt. Please go." Head bowed and voice choked, Lenora gazed down at her tanned hands, interlaced and writhing on her lap. She was lovely in the rose-colored gown with its low, tight bodice and flaring skirts.

"Let's dance, Len. I want to hold you."

"It wouldn't be any good, Curt, with all these people gaping at us and gabbing about us." Lenora scanned his profile, and reached over to caress his big, bruised hands. "You don't look bad—after the fight. I'm glad you beat Lyme—without having to shoot him."

"I'd still have to shoot him, and some of the others—if I stayed here. But I'm going away—tomorrow. I came to say good-by, Len."

159

She looked stricken. "It's probably best—the only thing to do. But I'll be lost without you, Curt."

"You'll be all right. You'll have Theron—If I don't kill him before I go."

"I don't want him anymore. I want you, Curt, no one but you."

"Well, I'll come back—sometime."

"Don't stay away too long. Don't make me wait too long." Her hands tightened on his, her dark eyes fixed and glowing on his scarred face. "But you must go now. It's better that you do, Curt darling."

"All right, Lenny. If that's what you want." He rose, stood in front of her, back to the dance floor, looking down at her with deep hunger and tenderness, a knot of pain filling his throat and making his eyeballs tingle. "So long, Len."

Curt saw the fear cross her brown eyes and fine features an instant before a hard fist sledged into the back of his neck, driving him forward over the chair he'd just vacated, his hands spread on the wall. Pushing off with his palms and spinning swiftly, he saw Theron Ware coming at him again with a murderous look in his eyes. Ducking beneath the flailing arms, Curt stabbed his left into Theron's face and poured all he had into a ripping right. He felt the mustache flatten under his fist and saw the blood spurt as Theron's glossy head jerked far backward.

Then a solid body landed on Curt's back, and powerful arms locked his elbows, pulling them back and pinning his arms securely. Butting back with his head and twisting his neck, Curt glimpsed the froglike features of Harry Keech, but he couldn't tear loose from those gorilla arms.

With Harry holding Curt tight and helpless, Theron Ware set himself and started smashing away in methodical fury at Curt's unprotected face. The blows came one on top of another, flogging Curt's head from side to side, sending streaks of light through his stunned brain—until Lenora Forbes flung herself upon Theron like a wildcat and clawed him back away from Curt. Harry Keech and other Frying Pan riders then rushed Curt across the waxed floor and hurled him headlong out into the corridor.

Falling to his hands and knees, Curt swayed there like a wounded animal, shaking his bent head to clear the fog and spattering drops of blood across the boards. Men were watching him from front and rear, but no one came near him. Doyle Guinness had herded Harry Keech and the other cowhands back into the dance hall.

When his head cleared and his strength began to return, Curt climbed to his feet, grabbed his hat and gunbelt off the wall peg, and staggered out of the building, down the steps, and on to the stone water trough. There he buried his head and face in the cool water time and again, washing off the blood and splashing about until he was somewhat restored and refreshed.

Conscious now of people watching him from a respectful distance, he dried hands and face on a clean handkerchief, set the hat on his wet head, and buckled on his gun. The music from the dance seemed to mock him, and Curt was in a stark killing mood as he started back toward the entrance of the town hall. There was but one thought in his throbbing head: *to kill Theron Ware and Harry Keech—and anybody else who got in his way.* Nothing but that mattered at this moment. He was all killer now.

But the tall, ramrod form of Stan Russett loomed suddenly before him, barring the way, and the deputy said sternly, "I'll take that gun, Curt. You've caused enough disturbance for one Saturday night."

"You'll play hell taking this gun," Curt said, through clenched teeth. "Get out of my way, Stan. I'm all through fooling around."

"You want me to run you in, Curt? I ought to, anyway, but I'll let you off—one more time."

"I'm warning you, Stan. Get the hell out of my way!"

"Look, Curt, I don't want to arrest you," Stan Russett said, with studied patience. "Even if you deserve it, boy. We was good friends once. Hand over that iron and go on home to bed."

"I'll keep the gun."

Russett was growing exasperated—a crowd was looking on and listening. "Damn it, Curt, you're getting to be a helluva nuisance in this town. Always fighting, always in trouble. Nothing but trouble wherever you go. You ought to be in jail. And you would be if Ed wasn't so softhearted."

Curt Metheny gestured in disgust. "I don't pick these fights, you damn fool. Parkhurst came after me, didn't he? Lyme Vector started it in the Ten-High. And just now Theron Ware slugged me while Harry Keech was holding me. You think I'm going to stand for that?"

"You'll have to, boy," Stan Russett said. "You had no business at the dance, anyway. You just went to start a ruckus. But you ain't going back in there to shoot anybody tonight."

Suddenly the fire burned out in Curt, leaving him empty, spent, and exhausted. "All right, Stan. I'll go home—*with* my gun. But tell Theron and Harry I'll be seeing them—real soon."

Russett's hawk-face hardened. "Keep on, Curt, and you're going to end up like your old—"

"Watch it, mister!" Curt cut in, with whiplike sharpness.

"I—I mean, you're going to end up bad, Curt, if you don't change your ways," Stan Russett said. "Go on back to the livery barn now and let folks enjoy this dance."

Curt smiled crookedly. "I said I was going. Don't push me, Stan."

"Go on then, for Godsake!" Russett motioned irritably, aware that this encounter was doing nothing to increase his stature in Holly Town. "Move along, damn it!"

Curt Metheny stared at him for a long scornful moment, then laughed softly and turned away.

Stan Russett drew, strode after him, and slashed the pistol barrel down on the back of Curt's hatted head. Curt felt it coming and tried to duck away, but his reflexes were dulled and late. His brain seemed to burst in a blinding white flash, and his legs melted beneath him. The ground rushed up at Curt as that brilliant light flickered and faded, and he never felt the earth against his face and chest.

When Curt rose slowly from fathomless depths of blackness, the dance was over, the music stilled, and the people gone. Warmly wrapped in blankets with a damp towel wound about his fevered head, he found he was lying on the grass near the carriage sheds behind the town hall. Pain splintered his head and blurred his vision; his face felt raw, gashed, and enormously swollen. There was little strength left in his limbs. He tried to sit up, and the pain rocketed behind his eyes. He sank back, sick and moaning.

Old Barnaby was sitting nearby, shoulders resting against the shed wall, a shotgun propped at his side, a bottle cradled in his lap. "Take it easy, son," he said, puffing on his pipe. "No hurry whatever. Lay back until you feel right."

Curt smiled faintly, comforted by the old man's presence. "It turned out to be—quite a ball, Barney."

"I won't say I told you so—even if I did." Barnaby grinned down at him. "You asked for it, Curt, and you got it. For a wonder your head ain't busted."

Planting his palms, Curt levered himself with slow care into a sitting position. Red rage erupted in him as he thought of Stan Russett and Theron Ware and Harry Keech, but it only increased his blinding headache. He put them out of mind and waited for the ground to stop tilting in under him.

"Theron and Harry came round to see you, Curt," said Barnaby, drinking from the bottle. "But they didn't linger long after I showed 'em this old Greener." He stroked the shotgun barrels fondly.

"A good thing you were here, Barney."

"There was others watching you before I got here," Barnaby said. "Maybe some folks are beginning to think you might be right, Curt, and the town might be wrong. They didn't care much for the way Stan Russett took you from behind."

"Stan always takes 'em from behind." Curt removed the towel and felt of the lump on his skull. "Have to let my hair grow if I'm going to get walloped on the head much," he said.

"You want a shot of this, son?" Barnaby held out the bottle.

"It might help some." Curt raised it to his sore mouth, and the brandy burned and spread a warm glow inside him.

After a while Curt got to his feet and moved about, limbering his cramped legs and arms, the earth still rocking and dipping beneath his boots. The Colt .44 was still in its sheath, and Barnaby got up and handed Curt his hat.

"Who owns the blankets and stuff?" Curt inquired.

"They're going to pick 'em up tomorrow after church. You feeling better?"

"I'm all right now, Barney. Go home and get some sleep."

"I'll walk to the stable with you," Barnaby offered.

Curt adjusted his hat and shook his head. "You've done enough. Go on home to bed, Barney. I can make it alone."

"Well, if you say so." Barnaby lifted his shotgun and extended the brandy bottle. "You want this, Curt? I've had enough."

"No thanks, you keep it. I've got that whiskey in the room."

Barnaby smiled at him. "See you in the morning, son."

"You bet, Barney," said Curt, smiling back at him. "And thanks for everything."

They separated then, Barney heading for Front Street, and Curt cutting across back lots toward the livery barn.

But Curt Metheny had overestimated himself. The strength began to seep out of his limbs before he had gone far, leaving him faint and giddy. His brain started spinning crazily, and weird visions floated shimmering in front of his eyes. He was sweating hard in the night coolness, with nausea coiling at the pit of his stomach.

Plunging erratically onward through the shadowy backyards, he saw the faces of his father and mother, his brother Jack and sister Amanda, and Curt wondered dimly if he was dying, if death was bringing them closer to him. It didn't matter much. He had little to live for.

Curt's head felt strange, and his sense of balance was awry. Once he ran into a clothesline and nearly fell backward. Again he slumped to his knees in a foul-smelling ash pile, and knelt there gagging for breath until he was able to rise and reel onward once more. Then something tripped him, and Curt was catapulted into a splay-legged running gait. He strove to recover his equilibrium, only to have the ground rise with sudden slamming force against his arms, chest, and body. He got up, panting and whimpering, to labor forward again on jerky trembling legs. But his eyes didn't work right; his arms and legs were no better; and nothing seemed real or natural.

At last he reached the barn, and fell against the wall. After resting a few minutes, he started working his way toward the rear. He had to force every movement as he rounded the corner and scraped along toward the back door.

The weakness and the sense of unreality were still with him. It was like a bad dream that came with a hangover, a nightmare from the fever swamps of delirium. The head injury must be worse than anyone had suspected. Curt had an eerie gone feeling, as if he were suspended in a vacuum. He felt numb and hollow, detached from life. Without panic or even fear, he thought of dying. Death seemed very near, and the faces of his dead parents and brother and sister swam once more before his eyes, clearer than anything else. He felt life ebbing out of him, and he did not care. He almost welcomed the release, the blessed flight to relief and freedom and nothingness.

Pushing off toward the back entrance, his goal finally within reach, Curt relaxed a trifle—and that was fatal. His mind blacked out; his knees gave way; and he rolled loosely into the deep shadow at the base of the barn wall, senses waning as he sank swiftly into endless depths.

THIRTEEN

When Curt came back to consciousness, uncertain of whether he was in the same world or a new one, his head and vision had cleared considerably. He heard the low murmur of nearby voices, and craned his neck to see the dark shapes of three men and three horses silhouetted against the starlit sky. The men were on foot, big and tough and gun-slung, with the alert look of the hunted about them. *Outlaws for sure,* Curt thought, and wondered if he was dreaming or dead. Things seemed clearer now; yet there was an unreal quality to everything.

"They ought to be here by this time, Utah," said one of the men, his voice harsh and rasping with impatience.

"Can't travel fast with Old Pitts so bad," drawled another, soft and mellow. "But they'll be along, Bowie."

Utah Tyrrell and Bowie Bowden, thought Curt, a cold chill spreading within him. *And the third man, tall and silent with a black-patched eye, was One-Eyed Jakes.* They had not seen Curt lying there in the black shadow at the foot of the wall. When they did, they'd probably start shooting—or use their gun barrels to keep it quiet. If they'd only give him a chance to talk first, it might work out all right.

"Old Pitts is dying, anyway," Bowie Bowden said. "But he's taking too long."

"A doctor might save him," Utah Tyrrell said, "if we could get hold of one. But we can't risk it here, with that job coming up. I saw our man here, and it's all set for Monday."

The bank, Curt thought. *They're going to hit this bank. And I'd give a lot to be with them when they do it.* He was feeling better, almost normal again, he discovered with astonishment. His brain was working right once more; his eyes were in focus; and his strength was returning.

"Naw, we can't get a sawbones in this town," Bowden said. "Can't take no chances, Utah. This one we gotta make good."

"It's too bad," Tyrrell murmured. "Pitts is a good man. Been with us a long time, Bowie."

"Yeah, sure, but his string run out. A risk we all run, Utah."

"He might make it yet. I never give up on a man. Not a man like Orson Pitts."

"A tough old coot," Bowden admitted. "But he's done for now. We should of ditched him back in the hills."

"No, Bowie," said Tyrrell. "Not as long as he's got a chance."

One-Eyed Jakes maintained his aloof and stony silence.

Curt wondered how he could announce his presence without getting shot up or gun-whipped.

Another gun-whipping would kill him as surely as a bullet. Probably the best way was to groan and stir around a bit, as if he were just coming out of it. That could be dangerous enough too, but he had to try something.

He began to moan and move slightly, like a man regaining his senses, and the three men wheeled swiftly toward him, guns leaping into their hands. Curt knew he'd never see three quicker draws.

"Hold it, boys," Utah Tyrrell said, coming forward, his pistol still ready. "The man's hurt."

"Drunk, you mean," scoffed Bowden. "I can smell him from here!"

One-Eyed Jakes spoke for the first time, in a tone of mild amusement: "You're disgusted, Bowie? You never got drunk, did you?"

Utah Tyrrell flipped his gun into his holster and crouched down, flicking a match alight on his thumbnail and cupping the flare in his palms. The tiny light flickered against Curt's bruised eyes, and Utah whistled softly. "Somebody did a job on this boy."

Curt blinked up at the man, seeing the birthmark dark and ugly on one side of the strong-boned face. "It took more than one of 'em," Curt muttered.

Utah Tyrrell smiled with pleasure, his eyes kind and friendly. "You're all right, kid. But what are you doing back here at this hour?"

"Work here," Curt said. "Live here. Couldn't quite make it home."

"You ought to see a doctor, boy."

"I don't need one."

"Maybe you could get a doc for us," Tyrrell suggested. "We've got a man coming who needs one bad."

Curt hitched himself up to sit propped against the wall. "Sure, I'll get Doc Pillon for you."

"Don't be a damn fool, Utah," broke in Bowie Bowden. "He'll bring back the law instead of a doctor. He knows there's money on our heads."

"Not me," Curt said, with a thin smile. "I've got no use for the law here. It was a deputy marshal busted me with a gun barrel. There'll be two or three dead men in Holly by tomorrow."

Bowie laughed. "Liable to be more'n that come Monday."

"I guess you know who we are," Utah Tyrrell said to Curt. "What's your name, son?" When Curt told him, it struck a chord in Utah's memory. "Metheny?" he mused. "Any relation to Judson Metheny, who raised a lot of hell hereabouts in the old days?"

"He was my father," Curt said simply.

In the background One-Eyed Jakes was beginning to take an interest for the first time.

Utah Tyrrell nodded with grave respect. "Old Jud was something. He sure put up one helluva battle against that posse in the Potholes. About ten years back, wasn't it? They still talk about it, all around this country. You feel able to go after the doctor now?"

"How do you know you can trust this punk, Utah?" demanded Bowie.

"I'm a pretty fair judge of men," Tyrrell said gently.

"No, Utah," grated Bowden. "This punk ain't going nowhere."

"Wait a minute here," One-Eyed Jakes said, shouldering past Bowie to step in and hunker down before Curt, an odd stare in that one good eye. "Well, damned! I should've known right away. Guess you don't recognize me, do you, kid?"

Curt regarded him with thoughtful care and wonder. "Am I supposed to? Thought there was something about you—but I can't place it."

Jakes smiled somberly. "Maybe you'd know me, Curt—if I wasn't wearing this patch."

Curt knew then, with a sense of stricken awe, a tingling of his spine. "*Jack!* For Godsake, Jack. We thought you were dead—at the Little Big Horn. Got a notice from the War Department and all. I can't hardly believe this, Jack. Why didn't Rita tell me?"

"I wouldn't let her, Curt. Made her promise not to—After what happened here, I figured it was better to stay dead."

"But how—?"

173

"I was with Reno up there instead of Custer," said Jack Metheny. "Lost an eye out of it, but didn't quite die. Listed first as Missing in Action. I let it ride that way, Curt—until they changed it to Dead."

"Jack, this is too much," Curt said as they clasped hands and hugged one another tight. "That night behind the Mustang—Barney and I both figured you was someone we ought to know."

Jack laughed softly. "So it was you and old Barney who took Theron off my back? Had an idea it might be. Theron tried to hire me to kill you that night, Curt. Imagine that? I damn near killed him instead."

"What the hell is this, anyway?" asked Bowie Bowden.

Laughing, Jack lifted Curt upright and turned to the others. "This is my kid brother Curt."

Utah Tyrrell reached out to shake Curt's hand, while Bowden stood back glaring and wagging his head. "Pleased to meet you, Curt," said Utah, and glanced quizzically at the elder brother. "So your real name is Jack Metheny."

"The secret's out, Utah," said Jack. "I hope you won't turn me in as a deserter from the U.S. Army."

"I'll have to give that some thought, Jack," said Utah, smiling. Curt thought it was the most winning smile he'd ever seen.

"Hey, they're coming," Bowie Bowden said, raising his hand. "Somebody is, anyway. Sounds like four-five horses out there."

Listening intently, they heard the faint slow *clop* of hoofbeats on the still night air, and then saw four horsemen emerge from the trees along the Ontawee River and move across the plain toward the livery barn. In the shadowy yard three riders swung down, the fourth remaining tied to his saddle and sagging in a lifeless posture.

"Where's the other horse, Kid?" inquired Utah Tyrrell of a slender, boyish rider.

"Had to shoot him—after Herm rode him almost to death. And Old Pitts is dead, Utah."

"Why the hell didn't you dump him then?" demanded Bowie Bowden.

"We don't dump men like Old Pitts," said the Kid, eyeing Bowie with distaste. "We bury them."

Bowden snorted loudly. "A helluva lot of difference it makes to a dead man! Herm, you oughta know enough to get rid of a corpse."

"I tried to, Bowie," mumbled the giant of the group. "They wouldn't do it, and I couldn't make 'em. They was two on one."

The stocky, bowlegged boy at the Kid's side laughed. "Herm was all for ditching Pitts till we offered to plant Herm right alongside the old man."

Bowden stared at the speaker. "Don't forget,

Dusty, the odds ain't two to one no more."

"Cut the foolishness," Utah Tyrrell commanded. "It's time to move out. Are you ready, Jack?"

"I want my brother to come with us, Utah," said Jack Metheny.

"The hell you say!" snarled Bowden. "We don't need a doctor no more, and we don't need any raw-necked recruit neither."

"Shut up, Bowie," said Utah. He looked steadily at the Metheny brothers. "You want the boy to turn outlaw, Jack?"

"No, I don't. But he isn't safe in this town, Utah. They're all gunning for him. I want him with me."

Utah turned his level gaze on Curt. "You sure you want to ride with us, son?"

"Yes, I'm sure," Curt said, his heart beating high and hard. Perhaps one of his dreams would come true, after all.

"He could help us a lot, Utah," said Jack. "Curt knows the bank and the town and the country outside a lot better than I do now."

"Well, it's all right with me," Utah Tyrrell said. "If it's agreeable to the rest. What do you say, boys?"

"Sure, Utah," said Kid Ansted, with an easy grin at Curt. "We can use another man. If he's Jakes's brother, that's good enough for me."

Dusty Shands nodded in confirmation. "Me too, Utah."

"All right, that gives us a majority," Utah Tyrrell said. "Get your horse and gear, Curt."

Herman Goedert remained silent and sullen, while Bowie Bowden spat, gestured, and grumbled, "One more way to split the pot! We don't need him any more'n we need Old Pitts's carcass, for Godsake!"

Inside the stable with Jack, Curt lit a lantern and led his big steeldust out of the stall as quietly as possible.

"This sure looks like home," Jack said, glancing around the cavernous interior. "Smells like it too, Curt. We had a lot of fun here, when we were kids—Show me your gear, and I'll saddle up while you're getting ready."

In his room Curt took off the store suit, white shirt, and fancy boots and got quickly into riding garb, with old spurred boots, leather vest, and brush jacket. He strapped on his gunbelt again, he took Parkhurst's .45, some extra boxes of shells, and the bottle of whiskey for his saddlebags. He hated to leave without saying good-by to little Tee Dee, Dane Lauritsen, and old Barney, but it couldn't be helped.

Jack had the big gray ready to go when Curt came out to latch on the saddlebags and place the Winchester in its sheath. Jack took a last look about the barn, then blew out the lantern and followed Curt and the horse through the back doorway into the night.

The others were waiting in the yard.

"Let's go, let's travel," rumbled Herm Goedert. "Before we wake up the whole damn town."

Kid Ansted sauntered over, slim and graceful, to shake Curt's hand, a smile dimpling his clean smooth cheeks. "Glad to have you with us, Curt. Quite a thing, you brothers getting together again after all these years."

Dusty Shands bowlegged it across to join them, a pleasant grin on his homely features as he greeted Curt and studied the gray gelding with admiration. "Welcome to our company, Curt. That's much horse you got there, as Spanish would've put it."

Bowden and Goedert made a point of ignoring Curt, with Bowie grumbling in an undertone.

"Don't let them two bother you any, Curt," said Kid Ansted. "They just naturally hate everybody—including themselves, I think."

They were about to mount when Utah Tyrrell lifted a hand and cocked his head. "Somebody's coming, boys. On the other side of the barn."

Curt dropped his reins as the rustling tread of boots in grass sounded nearer. "Let me handle this," he said, drawing his gun and pacing quietly toward the far corner of the building. "They know I belong here."

The stern voice of Stan Russett lashed out through the shadows: "What's going on out back there?"

"Nothing, Stan," Curt called back. "Just some late customers."

"That you, Curt? Why don't they use the front door?" Russett had stopped walking.

"Strangers, Stan. They came in the back way."

"I'll have a look at them," Russett said, coming on again.

Curt was silent, slipping nearer to the corner, not wanting to give away his position. The footsteps came closer, and Stan Russett came stalking into view, peering at the shadowy forms of men and horses in the back area.

As Stan moved toward them, Curt stepped out behind him and chopped down with the long barrel of his Colt. The jolt of the steel flattened Russett's hat and bent his head low, the shock vibrating through Curt's wrist and forearm. Stan grunted and lurched, took a faltering half-step, and floundered forward, pitching on full length face-down in the grass.

Curt picked up the lawman's pistol, holstered his own .44, and walked back to the waiting men. "The deputy," he said. "I owed him that one. And he'll get the full payment next time I see him."

"Stanko?" said Jack, smiling. "He ought to know better than to tangle with a Metheny."

"Cool and neat," Kid Ansted told Curt. Dusty Shands grinned and nodded his approval.

They mounted up and rode out at a walk, slow and quiet, toward the Ontawee crossing, with Kid

Ansted taking Old Pitts's horse on lead. Utah Tyrrell pulled over beside the Metheny brothers and asked Curt, "You know a good place to hide out?"

After pondering a moment, Curt remembered a narrow sunken canyon with an abandoned line shack and creek out in the broken wooded country toward the Sand Hills. He described it briefly, and Jack recalled the site, agreeing that it should serve their purpose.

Utah nodded in satisfaction and motioned them on ahead. "You two ride up front then. I know you've got a lot to talk about."

Riding with Jack at the head of the column, Curt felt happier than he had in years, although his head still ached dully and his face was sore and stiff. He was no longer alone. His big brother was back with him again. For the first time since his family had broken up, Curt Metheny really *belonged.*

Beyond the Ontawee River and out on the open, rolling prairie, Curt led them south and west toward the Sand Hills in the early morning hours. A light breeze stirred up alkali and brought the scent of sage, bunch grass, and wind-scoured earth and rock. The high plains were cut by creeks and coulees, with alders and cottonwoods fringing the water, and scrub cedars lining the cut banks of barren foothills. They passed an ancient buffalo wallow still littered with bleached bones, and saw in the distance the eroded chaos and volcanic desolation of the bad lands.

Curt and Jack had much to talk about, but the words didn't flow easily at the start. Jack spoke sketchily of the Little Big Horn, cavalry life in general, and the gun fighting and outlaw days that followed. Curt told awkwardly of the tragic end their mother and father had come to, and of his subsequent loneliness and misery in Holly Town.

"What kept you here, Curt?" asked Jack. "These last ten years must have been hell for you all alone."

"I don't know, Jack. Unless it was Lenora Forbes. She's always been the girl for me, like Rita has been for you."

"After we take this bank Monday, Rita and I are going away, Curt. We'll go somewhere new, and you're coming with us, Curt. We'll start a spread of our own, work it together, and build up a brand."

"If you really want me, Jack—you and Rita both."

"Of course we want you. We've always planned it that way, Curt," said Jack, with warm reassurance. "Rita thinks a lot of you. We've talked it all over a hundred times."

Curt shook his head. "I haven't got any money to put up."

"You don't need any. We've got plenty. Rita's been saving it for years."

"If I work the bank job with you, I'll get a split, won't I? I want something of my own to kick in."

"You better stay out of that," Jack said, his lips thinning.

"No, Jack, I want to be in on it. I've got to be. All my life I've wanted to hit that bank in Holly."

Jack's laugh was a trifle strained. "Well, we'll see, Curt. See what Utah thinks about it. But no matter what, we're going to be pardners from here on. And after we get set somewhere, you can come back after Lenora."

Curt felt a warm uplift in his breast, but his next thought cooled and dampened it. "Before I go, Jack, I've got to kill three men—maybe four."

"Forget it, Curt. It won't do any good, or make you feel any better." Jack's smile was bleak and mirthless. "I know, kid—because I've tried it."

"I can't forget it," Curt said. "It goes too deep, Jack."

"We'll wait and see what happens. The first thing to take care of is that bank. The bank that put Dad out of business."

"Who's your man in Holly Town?"

"I don't know—yet," Jack admitted. "Nobody knows but Utah. He'll tell us before we go in."

"I like Utah," said Curt, shyly. "And the Kid and Dusty."

"They're the best, Curt," agreed Jack. "They don't come any better."

"Never knew Old Pitts, but I feel bad for him."

Jack's laughter held a strange note. "Sometimes I feel sorry for everybody, kid. The living more than the dead. But Old Pitts was another good one."

In an interlude of silence, Curt thought how incredibly life could change in the space of a few hours. A short time ago he had thought he was dying, and it hadn't mattered much. Now he was fully alive, with so much to live for that death seemed remote, impossible. He had been all alone in a hostile world, beaten and broken, and then an old and hopeless dream had suddenly turned into reality.

He was riding with Utah Tyrrell's famous band, and his brother, miraculously returned from the dead, was riding at his side. The chance of striking back at Holly and its inhabitants was at hand. And Curt Metheny wouldn't have to go alone against the whole Ontawee country now.

FOURTEEN

In the early-morning darkness of Sunday, they reached the canyon and found the line cabin near the creek. Kid Ansted and Dusty Shands lowered the body of Old Pitts from his saddle. "We'll bury him in the daylight," Utah Tyrrell said as they hauled off saddle gear and turned the horses into the withered brush corral. Curt was tired enough to drop in his tracks, but he got out the quart bottle and passed it around.

Utah Tyrrell struck a match to inspect the shanty, and set a candle aglow in a bottle neck on the crude table. The camp was reasonably clean and sound, untenanted by pack rats or other animals, and there were two rawhide-slung bunks.

"You boys can draw lots for the beds, if you like," Utah said. "Rather sleep outside myself."

The Metheny brothers voiced a preference for the open air, with Kid Ansted and Dusty Shands following suit, and the shack was left to Bowie Bowden and Herm Goedert.

"I don't figure we need to set a watch," Utah Tyrrell said. "I sleep light, and so does Jack. The horses will sound off if anybody's coming."

"That deputy won't come to right away," Curt Metheny promised. "When he does, he won't be able to raise a posse this early on Sunday morning. Even if Ed Gracey would sanction raising one, which I doubt."

"No, Ed won't start a manhunt just because Stan got buffaloed," Jack said.

In the grass beneath tall cottonwoods, they bedded down in their blankets with saddles for pillows. It seemed good to Curt to sleep outdoors again, and he felt comfortable and secure with Jack beside him and the other three men close by. It was a relief to be separated from Bowden and Goedert. Exhaustion soon claimed him, dulling his aches and hurts, dragging him deep into slumber.

The sun, filtering through leafy boughs, awakened him at mid-forenoon, when it had climbed high enough to penetrate the narrow canyon. His headache had lessened, but his face and hands hurt worse than ever.

Jack Metheny and Utah Tyrrell were already up, washed clean with creek water, their bare heads glistening damply. Kid Ansted and Dusty Shands were still in their blankets, but they rolled out when Utah called, "Rise and shine, boys." With his towhead tousled and his cheeks flushed rosy from sleep, the Kid looked about fifteen years old, and the good-natured Dusty didn't look much older than that.

Curt saw what a distinguished-looking man Utah would have been if that purplish birthmark hadn't disfigured one side of his face. And even with his patched eye, Jack Metheny had a clean look of breeding and quality. One-Eyed Jakes, the notorious desperado and gun fighter—Curt's own brother, and Curt had never known it until last night.

The Kid and Dusty rousted Curt out of his blankets, romping and laughing like schoolboys. Bowden and Goedert came out of the cabin, sour-faced and sullen, glowering at the antics of the younger men with disgust.

"A damn bunch of nursery brats we got here," Bowie grumbled. "Wet-eared slicks and leppies. What do you think of that, Herm?"

"It's enough to turn a man's stomach, Bowie," growled Goedert.

The boys went down to the creek to wash up, a morning ritual that Bowie and Herm scorned to observe, and when they got back to camp, Utah had selected a site for the grave. Utah and Jack broke the ground and started digging with an old spade and shovel they had found rusting in the lean-to shed. After a while Bowie and Herm spelled them, and then the others took their turn at it. The hard, slow manual labor, which all riding men despise, started them sweating in the cool shade of the trees. Utah and Jack left to water and rub down the horses, while the rest went on with the gravedigging chore.

"We oughta let the new boy do all the digging, Herm," declared Bowden as they watched Curt and Dusty toil away. "He's real handy with that shovel."

"Sure, Bowie, all he ever done was shovel out stables," Goedert said. "With all that practice the boy's bound to be good."

"That's what we needed most, a good shovel man," Bowie said. "We was sure lucky to find this one. With him, we'll take that bank like nothing."

Spade in hand, Dusty Shands turned on Bowden. "Shut your trap, Bowie! Before I shut it with this spade."

"Let 'em rave, Dusty," said Curt Metheny. "It don't bother me."

Bowie and Herm kept up the baiting and heckling until Jack Metheny returned from the corral. Then it ceased abruptly. Maybe they weren't afraid of Jack, thought Curt, but they sure had plenty of respect for him—and for Utah Tyrrell.

It was a bright, clear morning, a beautiful day to be alive, and Curt felt a pang of pity and sorrow for Old Pitts, who was beyond seeing this blue sky and feeling the golden sunshine.

They were all relieved when Utah came back to examine the rectangular hole in the ground, and said, "That's deep enough, boys."

The blanket-wrapped body was lowered in with care, and the men stood around for a moment of silence. Then, as quickly as possible, they filled the grave with raw reddish dirt, and Utah Tyrrell replaced the sods with meticulous care. All hands helped cover the spot with rocks, and Old Pitts was gone forever.

"Well, the old man's got a pretty place to rest in," Kid Ansted murmured, blowing sweat off his upper lip.

"Yeah, he'll really enjoy it here, Kid." With a snort, Bowden wheeled away toward the line shack. "Let's get some breakfast on the fire."

Herm Goedert tramped ponderously after Bowie and, watching them, Curt knew there was no mercy, no sympathy, in that pair. Goedert, an insensate brute, felt nothing at all. And Bowie didn't care who died as long as he remained alive himself.

The others, lingering quietly at the grave, felt a grief that was deep and real. And Curt Metheny, who had never seen Orson Pitts alive, shared it with them. When Curt walked away with Dusty and the Kid, Jack and Utah were still standing in silence over the rock-cairned mound.

While breakfast was being prepared by Utah and Jack, the three younger men went back to the creek and stripped down this time to plunge into the pure running water and splash and swim about until they felt glowing clean and refreshed. It was like boyhood days, Curt thought, reveling in the cool rush of the current as it rippled along its stony bed and spun lacy froth about the protruding boulders. There was a ledge over a deep pool, and one after another Curt and the Kid and Dusty dived from it, exulting in the winged flight through space and the pleasant shock of striking the water.

Sun-dried and dressed once more, they ate with ravenous appetites, and afterward the boys washed the few cooking and eating utensils while Utah and Jack shaved and bathed in the stream. Bowie and Herm lazed around, smoking and talking in low voices, content to remain beard-stubbled and filthy in their trail-worn clothing, rank with sweat.

Sunday afternoon they spent lounging about camp and plotting their campaign against the bank in Holly Town. Utah had a rough map of the area and a detailed chart of the bank interior, which they studied carefully while Curt Metheny sketched out the street system of Holly in Utah's notebook, locating additional places and land-marks at the prompting of Jack and Utah.

"A good job," Utah approved, scanning Curt's chart, and then his face. "How far do you want to go with us, Curt?"

"All the way," Curt said, without hesitation.

Utah glanced at Jack, who shrugged and nodded slowly, saying, "That's what he wants, Utah. I couldn't talk him out of it."

Utah looked at the others. "What do you boys say?"

The Kid and Dusty responded with instant nods and smiles, and Curt knew he was in, regardless of the minority opposition. Bowie Bowden spoke for himself and Goedert:

"We don't like it—but we can't do nothing about it. You got the vote. And by now the punk knows so much we can't turn him loose, so we got to drag him along. If he queers it, well, he queers it, that's all."

"All right, Curt, you ride with us," Utah Tyrrell said, and went on to outline their course of action and each man's assignment, going over it time and again until it was sharply imprinted in everyone's mind.

"That bank'll be loaded tomorrow," Utah told them. "More money than it ever held before at one time. We should be set for a long while, boys, if we pull this one off right." Then he plotted their escape route, if all went smooth and well, adding, "If something goes wrong, if we have to break up and scatter, we'll rendezvous at Lodestone." He pointed out the ghost town on the map.

"Utah would've made a great field officer," Jack whispered aside to Curt. "We could've used him on the Little Big Horn."

"Can we trust that inside man?" Bowie Bowden wanted to know.

"Don't see how he can cross us—unless he wants to die," Utah Tyrrell said. "He's going to be there. If he tries to pull anything, he'll get the first bullet."

Curt was trying to figure out who the inside man might be. There were no very likely suspects, it seemed. But then, Curt didn't know much about the bank employees, except for Barnaby and Theron Ware. If it were Barney, he would have told Curt about it—wouldn't he? If it were Theron, why had he tried to shoot Jack that night in back of the Mustang?

"I want two men in town tonight," Utah said. "That'll be the Kid and Dusty—they look the least like bad men." He touched his blemished cheek and smiled at Jack's eye patch. "You and I are too easy to recognize, Jack—and Bowie and Herm look too tough."

"Why don't we all go in together in the morning?" Bowden asked.

"That way we might run into another Arrowhead. This way the Kid and Dusty can warn us off if there's anything like that brewing."

"They better stay sober," Bowie muttered, his eyes narrowed on Ansted and Shands.

"Don't worry about that, Bowie," laughed Kid Ansted. "Saloons are the first place you and Herm head for in any town, but Dusty and I got more sense."

Utah Tyrrell turned to Curt. "You'd probably like to go in tonight, too. Pick up some of your things and get ready to move out." Curt nodded, and Utah continued: "You'll have to stay out of sight—and out of trouble."

"I will," Curt promised earnestly. "I won't leave the livery barn."

Bowie Bowden exploded: "For the luvva god, Utah! This punk's liable to give the whole damn thing away."

"I don't believe so," Utah said quietly.

Jack Metheny fixed his one eye coldly on Bowden. "Keep your tongue off my brother, Bowie. I won't bother to warn you again."

Bowie got up and stalked away from the circle, with Herm Goedert lumbering along behind him.

"It smells some better with them two polecats gone," Dusty Shands remarked, with a homely grin.

Utah shook his gray-streaked dark head. "Ever since Arrowhead, they've been hard to live with."

"Tomorrow'll make up for that, Utah—and more," Kid Ansted said, inclining his sunny head in sober assurance.

Jack eyed his brother. "Don't try to settle any personal scores in there tonight, Curt—or tomorrow either. They'll have to wait."

"That's right, son," Utah Tyrrell said as Bowden and Goedert drifted back in and sank to the turf. "We don't kill unless we have to. I want you all to bear that in mind—you in particular, Bowie. You know you didn't have to shoot that agent in Wallace."

"He coulda had a hide-out gun, and I woulda been as dead as Old Pitts is now," Bowden said. "It's a lot safer to shoot and make sure of 'em, Utah."

"I don't want any shooting—unless it's absolutely necessary." There was an icy edge to his mild voice. "Understand that, Bowie?"

"Yeah, sure, all right, Utah," mumbled Bowden. "You're the boss man. But we're all wanted for murder—remember?"

"That doesn't give us the license to kill any more," Utah Tyrrell said. "Don't ever forget that, Bowie."

Late in the afternoon, as Curt Metheny was saddling up with Kid Ansted and Dusty Shands, Utah eased in beside him. "Curt, are you dead sure you want to come in with us? Don't do it, son, unless you're real sure."

Curt nodded his sandy head. "I'm sure, Utah. There's nothing else for me in Holly—or anywhere else that I know of."

"All right, Curt." Utah held out his hand. "See you tomorrow."

"You want to tell me who the inside man is?" Curt inquired as they shook hands.

Utah smiled. "Why not? It's Theron Ware. You know him, of course."

"I know him all right. But I don't like him, Utah—or trust him."

Jack Metheny had come up to join them. "Did you say Theron Ware?" he asked. "He wouldn't admit to me he was our man that night I was in town. And he would've shot me in the back if Curt and old Barney hadn't opened up on him. What kind of an inside man is that—? Maybe he just wanted the reward money on me."

Utah Tyrrell frowned in deep perplexity. "I can't understand that. And I don't like it—not a damn bit. But it's too late to do anything about it now. We'll just have to watch Ware close tomorrow. He'll be in there—under our guns." Utah walked off, his head bowed in somber contemplation.

Jack gripped his brother's hand. "Rita's going to be waiting for me in Lodestone tomorrow afternoon, Curt. If anything should happen—go wrong or something—you know. Not that it will, but just in case—Well, you meet her and take care of her."

"Sure, Jack, but you'll be there," Curt said, feeling coldness spread in the pit of his stomach. "It can't go *that* wrong, Jack."

"Of course not, kid." Jack Metheny smiled brightly. "I'll be there, sure. We'll ride out together—the three of us."

Jack turned back to camp, and Curt swung up on the tall steeldust, sorely troubled and deeply afraid. Dusty and the Kid were already in their saddles, and they rode out in the direction of Holly Town.

194

The stars came out bright and glittering and the moon rose with golden-red glory in the eastern sky behind the town as the three riders split up to make their separate entrances to Holly Town. Curt forded the shallows in the Ontawee, and thought of that night with Lenora Forbes under those trees. He'd have to try and forget her, now that he had become an outlaw. He crossed the flats and reached the back door of the livery barn, unnoticed in the long-shadowed darkness.

He was unsaddling in the stable when Tee Dee came along and hailed him with happy delight. "You all right, Curt?" he asked. "I was afraid they'd killed you, but Barney swore you was alive somewhere."

"Sure, I'm okay, Tee Dee," said Curt, hanging up his saddle gear.

"I'll rub him down for you, Curt," offered Tee Dee. "I like to work on this big gray. I sure missed you, Curt. This place is nothing, when you ain't here."

Dane Lauritsen overtook Curt before he reached his room. His greeting was less enthusiastic than Tee Dee's.

"Where you been all day, Curt?" he asked, his thin face lined and gloomy behind the cold cigar and the yellow mustache.

"Resting up, Dane. I got hurt a little last night."

"Yes, I heard all about it," Lauritsen said dryly. "I guess it's hopeless, isn't it?"

"I guess so, Dane. I'm going away pretty soon now."

"Maybe that's best. Either you won't change, or the town won't let you. Almost anywhere else ought to be a lot better for you."

"I know, Dane," said Curt. "I should've gone long ago."

"Well, you own your horse and saddle and gear. I'll give you your wages and a stake to get started on, Curt."

"Just the wages. I won't need any stake. You've done enough for me, Dane."

Lauritsen bit deep into the cigar and spread his bony hands. "It's too bad, son, and I'm sorry. I hoped it would work out for you—for us both here. But it don't seem to, and I guess it never would." He sighed and turned away, then halted abruptly. "Stan Russett's been looking for you all day, Curt."

"Don't tell him I'm here, Dane," said Curt Metheny. "If he comes after me, I'll probably have to shoot him. Don't tell anyone I'm here except old Barney."

"All right," agreed Lauritsen, moving on toward his office.

Curt stretched out on his bunk and stayed there all day. Tee Dee brought him supper from the Greek's, without whiskey—Curt didn't want to be hung over or half-sick or primed with any false courage tomorrow. It was going to be the greatest day in his life—it was going to wipe out all the shame and humiliation and sorrow of the past years—and Curt wanted to be right and ready for it.

It meant giving up Lenora Forbes, losing her forever, but that couldn't be helped now. She was beyond his reach, anyway. A man could hardly expect both of his big dreams to come true. If just one of them did, he was far more fortunate than most people.

After supper that evening, Curt's last in the cell-like room that had been his home for years, he packed and checked and overhauled his gear for the trail while chatting with old Barnaby and little Tee Dee. He found a left-hand holster, and Tee Dee rigged it on his shell belt to carry the .44 he had taken from Stan Russett. The .45 that belonged to Alvah Parkhurst would go back in the saddlebags after Curt and Barney finished cleaning and oiling all the guns.

Dane Lauritsen brought Curt's pay in an envelope, and on opening it to return the five to Barnaby, Curt saw that Dane had added a hundred-dollar bonus, with a note insisting that Curt keep it.

As usual, Barnaby had a little news, which he delivered in a rambling fashion: "Parkhurst ain't telling where he got that money, but Ed Gracey's still working on him. There's a rumor going round that Utah Tyrrell's gang is in the Ontawee country now. Stan Russett was hunting high and low for you all day, Curt, but Ed told him to lay off and forget it tonight. They say that Lenora Forbes broke off her engagement to Theron Ware and swore she'd shoot Theron if he came out to Frying Pan to see her—"

Once that would have been the very best kind of news to Curt Metheny, but now it meant little or nothing. Lenora Forbes was already lost to him, regardless of how she felt about Theron Ware. After one farewell drink with old Barney, Curt got ready for bed.

At the doorway Barnaby paused to say good night. "I'm going to miss you, boy. It ain't going to be the same here. But I know you got to go."

"If things work out, Barney, I'll send for you," Curt said, smiling fondly at the old man. "And maybe you can bring Tee Dee, too."

FIFTEEN

Monday morning was gray and overcast, with a gusty wind carrying the threat of rain. Curt, his steeldust gelding saddled and ready for the trail, said good-by to Dane Lauritsen, Tee Dee, and the other hostlers. It brought a painful lump up in his throat when little Tee Dee burst out crying, and Dane turned away blinking and gulping, the unlit cigar bobbing under his grayish-yellow mustache.

Curt rode leisurely out the drive to Front Street and turned toward the bank. Hat cocked on his tawny head, he wore a dark blue shirt with a gray scarf and leather vest, bleached blue denim pants cuffed on spurred half-boots, and the double-sheathed gun harness. Behind the cantle was lashed his bedroll, slicker, and brush jacket; from the pommel hung a canteen and coiled rope; and the Winchester jutted butt-up from its saddle scabbard. The saddlebags were loaded with extra clothing and cartridges, Parkhurst's .45, some sandwiches, tobacco, and a bottle of brandy, which Barney and Tee Dee had presented to him.

Good-by, Holly Town, mused Curt Metheny. *I'll soon be gone—but not forgotten. After today, this town won't ever forget me.*

The wind blew grit and sand against the false fronts and board overhangs, rattling shutters and setting signs asway. People along the street turned to watch the lean rider on the big gray horse.

Other riders and wagons raised dust along Front Street, and loafers idled as usual under wooden awnings, with horses switching flies at the hitchracks before them. Housewives, out to do their daily shopping, gossiped with one another and the storekeepers, and men along the way watched the wind blow and tug at the women's skirts. It was just like any other forenoon in Holly, and this was difficult for Curt Metheny to accept and believe. He had the queer feeling that his intentions must be obvious, that anyone could tell at a glance he was on his way to help rob the bank, and he wondered why the alarm didn't rise and spread.

It was nearing ten-thirty, the appointed time, when Curt reached the adobe-block bank building. Five horses were racked on the River Street side of the bank, four with saddles and Old Pitts's mount rigged with packs. On the corner Kid Ansted and Dusty Shands sat their broncs with casual ease, in position to cover both streets and the bank entrance.

The Kid, his hair shimmering golden under his hat, was smoking a long, thin cigar, which looked absurdly out of place in his boyish face. Dusty, a chew of tobacco warping one brown cheek, was grinning that homely, pleasant grin of his. They paid no attention to Curt as he swung into River Street, stepped down, and tied the gray beside the other five horses.

At exactly ten-thirty Curt walked into the bank and took his allotted stand by the door, his throat choking dry and his heart hammering at his ribs. The others were already in their places, deeper within the gloomy interior. Utah Tyrrell wore a slicker, the collar turned high to conceal his birthmarked cheek, and Jack Metheny's hatbrim was pulled low over his patched eye. Big Goedert and Bowie Bowden slouched indolently at the center of the room.

There were four customers at the grilled counter, all men and packing pistols, with two clerks in attendance behind the grille. J. A. Cottrell, puffing on a fat cigar, sat lumpily behind his elaborate desk in the background. Theron Ware was nowhere in sight, and that worried Curt— until he remembered that Theron was to be back in the vault to assist Bowden with the big money there.

Stifling an impulse to yawn from the nervous strain, Curt was almost as startled as the clerks and customers when Utah Tyrrell's cool, easy voice broke the stillness: "Don't move, anybody. This is a holdup. Nobody gets hurt if you all keep quiet and do as you're told. Anyone that reaches gets it." The outlaw guns came out, Curt drawing automatically with the rest, and the arms of the clients, the clerks, and J. A. Cottrell went up toward the ceiling.

Jack Metheny quickly herded the four customers out of the way and lined them up facing the side wall, near a door that opened into the alley there. One after another, Jack flipped the guns from those holsters into the large pockets of his brush jacket.

The two clerks and J. A. Cottrell stood with upraised arms, gaping in stricken terror at all the guns covering them, too scared to even notice Curt's presence among the bandits. Bowie Bowden pushed through the gate into the employees' side and strode toward the vault at the rear. Herm Goedert, following Bowie into the enclosure, set the clerks to emptying their cash drawers into canvas bags. Utah Tyrrell and Curt Metheny watched the proceedings over leveled pistol barrels, with Curt splitting his vision to keep the front entrance under observation, while Jack Metheny continued to hold his four captives against the side wall.

"Get 'em outside, Jack, and hold 'em in the alley," Utah said. "Might as well clear this room."

Jack promptly prodded the four men outside under his guns, and the door swung shut behind his rangy form. Instantly feeling the loss of his brother, Curt fought down the cold clutch of momentary panic. Without Jack, he felt alone again.

When J. A. Cottrell started forward, uttering a strangled squawk of protest, Bowie Bowden whirled from the vault entrance and swung his gun barrel, knocking the bank president flat and senseless on the floor. Turning to the doorway again, Bowie spoke sharply to someone inside the vault.

Everything was going slick as grease, and Curt thought it was ridiculously simple to stand up a bank if you knew your business as this crew did. Goedert had his canvas sacks nearly filled, and Bowden was collecting other bags from the main treasury. In a few fleeting minutes the job was practically done.

Then a rear door opened, and old Barnaby emerged in all innocence, gray head bent and oblivious as he shuffled forward carrying a cardboard box full of waste paper, wholly unaware of the situation he had walked into. Barney angled toward the side door, and Curt thought thankfully: *He'll be all right out there with Jack.* But Bowie Bowden turned from the vault and spotted the old man.

"Hold on there, grampaw!" barked Bowie. "Stop where you are."

Barnaby, hearing nothing, stumped on toward the side exit, and Curt thought with freezing despair: *This does it. I can't let him shoot old Barney. I won't let that happen. Even if it costs my life.*

"Let him go, Bowie," called Curt. "He's all right. He just can't hear."

Disregarding Curt, Bowden yelled furiously: "Hold it, you damn old fool! Come on back here!" He lined his pistol at Barnaby's stooped plodding back, and Curt saw that Barney wasn't wearing a gunbelt.

"No, Bowie, no!" Curt cried, in desperation. "Don't shoot him. He's deaf, Bowie, he's deaf!"

But Bowden was going to fire. It showed in his evil eyes and ugly features, the lust to kill. Curt lined his right-hand Colt and let go, the flame spearing slantwise over the grilled counter, the .44 jerking up hard in his hand. The bullet punched into Bowie's neck, under the jawbone, twisting his head and slamming him back against the doorframe of the vault. He hung there, a flood of crimson staining his chest, and strained to raise his gun toward Curt, his eyes glaring madly.

"I told you, Utah," panted Bowie. "That punk—" He pitched forward with a choking cough, his pistol exploding as he struck the floor, and squirmed into stillness beside the unconscious bulk of J. A. Cottrell. The two gun blasts filled the room and shivered the windows, setting a crystal chandelier atinkle overhead.

Barnaby had turned and seen what was going on for the first time, his faded eyes lighting at the sight of Curt Metheny out by the front door, a gun smoking in his right hand. Obeying an old gun fighter's instinct, without thought or hesitation, Barney crouched to set down the carton of waste and lunged along the floor toward the pistol that had bucked loose from Bowie Bowden's dying grasp.

Herm Goedert had wheeled instantly within the cage to fire at Metheny, and Curt felt the scorching suction of the slug past his left shoulder as he thumbed a shot back into that blinding muzzle flash. It struck home solid, breaking the giant at the waist and driving him back upon a desk. Lurching off the wood on sagging knees, his unaimed weapon blaring once more to splinter a wall panel behind Curt, Herm Goedert toppled and crashed full length on the boards, his massive hulk settling into an inert, shapeless sprawl.

Then Curt Metheny turned to Utah Tyrrell and saw Utah's guns already bearing full upon him—and wondered why Utah hadn't shot him down long before now. The initial surprise and anger had gone from Utah's clean gray eyes, and there was a strange look of resignation and under-standing on his face. Curt held his own fire, the hammers back under his thumb joints, unwilling to shoot this man.

"The old man, a friend of yours," Utah murmured. "Funny how things happen—Bowie's fault, of course."

Smiling faintly with regret, Utah Tyrrell

swerved his right-hand barrel slightly. Flame lanced from it, and a hammer blow smashed Curt's left arm, jarring and spinning him halfway round, flinging him back on the wall. He rested there shocked and numb, feeling nothing except wonder, the pistol dropping from his left hand. Curt could not, or would not, lift his right-hand gun against Tyrrell—any more than Utah could fire at him again. Frozen motionless there, they stared at one another for long sick seconds, neither man wanting to kill the other.

It was then that old Barnaby, bent only on helping and saving Curt Metheny, reared up off his knees behind the counter and fired Bowie's pistol through the grillwork at Utah Tyrrell, the slug turning and jolting Utah into the only awkward move Curt ever saw him make.

Beaten back against a high wall-desk, Utah drooped there, his arms hanging low as if the guns were suddenly too heavy, his bowed head rocking wearily from side to side. "I knew it," Utah said, soft and distinct. "I knew it, all the time—" Gunflame from old Barney's hand stabbed at him again, and Utah Tyrrell folded in the middle, fell to his knees, and slid forward onto his face, to lie unstirring beneath the reeking swirl of powder smoke.

Retching sick with his wounded left arm dangling, Curt Metheny moved unsteadily toward the front door, wanting to warn his brother Jack and Kid Ansted and Dusty Shands. He did not see Theron Ware come out of the vault and club old Barney down under a pistol barrel and stare menacingly through the gunsmoke at Curt's back.

Reeling out on the slat walk, Curt saw the Kid and Dusty, their youthful faces drawn bleak and grim, still sitting their nervous, prancing horses at the corner. But Jack wasn't anywhere in sight.

"Ride for it, boys," Curt told them. "All dead in there. Never mind about me. Ride out while you can."

"Aren't you coming with us, Curt?" asked Kid Ansted.

Curt shook his head. "Can't ride—with this arm."

"But they'll get you, Curt," said Dusty Shands.

"No, I'm all right. They don't know I was in it. Get going, for Godsake!"

Bewildered and reluctant, but aware of men swarming toward the bank from all directions, Kid Ansted and Dusty Shands wheeled away on their broncs and raced out River Street at a gallop, the dust billowing high behind them. They might make it. Curt hoped so. They had a chance, at any rate. But where was Jack?

The pain started in Curt's arm then, the intensity of it leaving him faint and ill. He clawed at the hitch rail, missed it, and fell flat on the gritty planks of the sidewalk, just in time to escape the bullet that whipped over him with a vicious whine.

Stan Russett, leading a pack of men out Front Street toward the bank, had fired that shot at Curt and cursed as he saw it miss. Stan was about to throw down again at Curt's prone figure when Jack came out of the alley beside the bank, calling: "Try this Metheny, Stanko. This one's standing up."

Shocked to a sudden halt and twisting round to face this new threat, Russett gasped: *"Jack Metheny!"* And his eyes bulged in horror at the sight of this ghost, a man risen from the grave, as Stan swung his gun frantically in Jack's direction.

With a cold smile, Jack Metheny opened fire, slashing out his first shot before Russett could trigger, and then blasting away so fast that the concussions blended into one vast roar. The lead lifted Russett tall and lashed him backward in a long, stilted stagger, across the boardwalk into the street, his rawboned frame shuddering under each impact. He went down wallowing in the deep gravel, and dust geysered from his riddled body as Jack pumped a final shot into it. The men behind the deputy had broken and fled to cover, and Jack turned toward his fallen brother.

"There's one punk Curt won't have to kill," Jack said, holstering the empty Colt and pulling a loaded one out of his jacket pocket.

Curt had reached up to the hitchrack and hauled

himself upright with his good arm. Now he was leaning back against the rail, dimly aware that Jack had emptied a gun into Stan Russett, and a crowd had gathered to look on from a safe distance. It had all happened too fast to seem real and true, a lifetime of violence compressed into a few flaming minutes. Curt was facing the bank, gun hanging in his right hand, when Jack came to a stop in front of him.

"Got held up," Jack said. "Those depositors tried to jump me, and I had to flatten a few heads. You hit bad, Curt?"

"No, I don't think it's broke," Curt said, glancing at his blood-soaked left arm. "You've got to get out of here, Jack. Get on your horse and ride."

"What about you, kid?"

"I'm in the clear, Jack," said Curt, and told him how it had gone inside the bank.

"Utah, too?" Jack groaned. "What luck."

"Jack, will you for Godsake get started and light out?" Curt panted, with frenzied urgency.

Jack smiled tautly. "All right, Curt, I'll see you—"

Gunfire streaked out from the bank entrance, and Curt heard the slug thump into Jack's back. The shock threw Jack forward against his brother, surprise and disgust mirrored in his one eye, and Curt reached out one-handed to catch and hold him. "Don't that beat hell?" Jack said, with a wan, ironical grin. "Tell Rita—" Then he was falling backward, too heavy for Curt's right arm to hold, crashing down across the walk at Curt's feet, with dust spurting up thinly between the sun-bleached slats. Jack was dead when he hit the planks, and Curt knew it. But there was no time for grief.

Curt had glimpsed Theron Ware inside the bank doorway, and he raised his gun into line, but Theron faded from sight before Curt could squeeze the trigger. Pushing himself off the rack, Curt stepped carefully over Jack's body and started for the entrance, but his legs were weak and erratic, and the distance seemed great. He had to kill Theron Ware. He had to get inside those adobe walls before someone else started shooting at him from the street. *Jack was dead.* He had found Jack only to lose him again, and this time it was final and forever.

Behind Curt, Ed Gracey had come to crouch down and examine the bodies of Stan Russett and One-Eyed Jakes, while a curious crowd closed in to cluster about the dead men, in defiance of Gracey's profane orders to stand back and show a little human decency and respect.

When Curt Metheny finally made it into the powder stench of the bank interior, sick enough to vomit but gagging it back, holding it down, Theron Ware was gone. The dead lay where they had fallen, Utah Tyrrell on the main floor, Herm

Goedert and Bowie Bowden within the enclosure. J. A. Cottrell was seated at his desk once more, head clasped in both hands, with the two clerks hovering anxiously over him, apparently unable to do anything to ease, comfort, or please the president. Barnaby was slumped heavily on the counter, with blood smearing his gray hair, and Curt went straight to him.

"Where's Theron, Barney?"

"I don't know, Curt. Gone, I guess—Did you get it bad, boy?"

"Just creased my arm," Curt said. "What happened to you?"

"Theron come up from behind and bent a gun over my head. I was afraid he'd get you in the back."

"He got Ja—Jakes," said Curt, wincing with teeth on edge as the pain washed brightly through his left arm. It brought the sweat out in large beads, and left him dizzy, faint, and sick to his stomach.

"Lemme see that arm, Curt," said Barnaby. "It's bleeding like hell."

Curt slid through the gate in the waist-high partition and slumped down in a chair, weak and tired, feeling the pain go in and out of his torn arm. Barnaby rolled up the shirt sleeve to inspect the wound and got a bandage out of the bank's medical kit to stanch the blood.

"It ain't bad, Curt, but it must hurt some,"

Barnaby said as he swabbed. "Don't think it touched the bone."

"I got to get Theron Ware," said Curt. "Where'd he go?"

"Must of gone out the back way—"

Ed Gracey entered and surveyed the smoky interior, then fixed a penetrating gaze on Curt and gestured at the dead men on the floor. "You know them, Curt? Who are they?"

"Well, I can name them, Ed." He indicated one body after another. "Utah Tyrrell—Herm Goedert—Bowie Bowden."

"And One-Eyed Jakes out front. How many got away?"

Curt shrugged and shook his head.

"What were you doing with them, boy?" Ed Gracey demanded.

Curt stayed silent, and one of the clerks spoke up: "Curt wasn't with them, Marshal. He broke up the whole thing. Curt killed two of them, and Barney shot the other one."

"All right, Curt," said Gracey patiently. "Tell me what happened."

"I took Bowden and Goedert first. Utah hit me in the arm, and Barney busted him. Then outside, Jakes got Russett—and Theron Ware shot Jakes in the back."

"Just like that," the marshal drawled, with irony. "So Theron Ware's a hero too, along with you and Barney?"

"I suppose so." Curt let it go that way. He wanted Theron for himself.

Gracey glanced down at Curt's arm. "Let me have a look at that, Barney. Doc Pillon's on his way here."

Curt Metheny lay back in the chair, bathed in sweat as he fought the fiery anguish that was eating into his arm, and Ed tightened the tourniquet that Barnaby had fashioned.

"There are rewards out on those four men," Ed Gracey said. "At least five thousand on Utah Tyrrell. Two or three thousand on the others. Total of from eleven to fourteen thousand dollars maybe."

"I never gave that any thought," Curt said, in all honesty.

Ed Gracey smiled down at him. "I know that, Curt. You're no bounty hunter, and neither is Barney. But that money's coming to you. And it's about time you got a break in this country."

"We'll split it then," Curt Metheny said. "Barney got the big one, you know. Barney got Utah Tyrrell."

"At my age money don't mean a whole lot," Barnaby said, with a grave smile. "But I'm sure glad for Curt's sake. You got your life ahead of you, Curt. And it ought to be a lot better life the rest of the way, son."

With the tourniquet tight and the bleeding stopped, numbness came back to blot out the agony in Curt's arm.

"Where's that damn Doc Pillon?" grumbled Ed Gracey. "If he gets much slower, he'll have to turn undertaker."

Barnaby placed a well-rolled cigarette in Curt's mouth and lit it for him. The smoke tasted nice and soothing, even in his parched mouth. Curt wondered at the freakish twists that fate took. Setting forth to be an outlaw this morning, he had wound up a local hero, with thousands of dollars in reward money coming to him and Old Barney. Theron Ware would never collect his share for killing Jack. Theron was going to die for that—and for other reasons.

"We can start up a spread of our own, Barney," said Curt, and thought of Jack with a desolate, wrenching pang of grief and loss and sorrow. "You and Tee Dee and I."

"Sure, Curt, that's what we'll do," Barnaby agreed, a smile lighting his sunken eyes and leather cheeks. "You and me and little Tee Dee, with a layout of our own."

And a home for Rita, too, Curt was thinking. Perhaps Lenora Forbes would share it, as his wife. Yes, there was a chance of his other dream coming true, now that this one had ended as it did—

Ed Gracey bent down and spoke softly: "You want to take care of any of these bodies, Curt?"

Curt Metheny realized then that Ed Gracey knew about Jack, and also that the secret would be safe with the marshal.

"Yes, Ed," he murmured. "I'll take Jakes—and Utah Tyrrell."

Ed Gracey, his features rocklike once more, stared about the bank in mild disgust. "Ain't this one helluva mess, though?" he said morbidly. "Five dead men on a Monday morning, in the town where I'm supposed to keep law and order."

Curt smiled thinly at the irony of Ed's words, the irony of fate and life.

A cry of mortal anguish rose in the background, and they turned to see what had caused it. J. A. Cottrell, flanked by his clerks, was standing at the entrance of the vault, and the sound was coming from him:

"The money's gone! The money from the vault! A fortune, I tell you, a fortune! Come here, Marshal, don't just sit there. They cleaned out the vault, and I'm ruined, ruined!"

Ed Gracey squinted at Curt and Barney. "I thought the outlaws didn't take a thing."

"They didn't," Curt said, and Barnaby nodded in agreement.

"Who the hell got away with it then?"

Curt Metheny shrugged, his lean face masked and expressionless. "Must've been somebody on the inside, Ed. An employee, maybe."

Ed Gracey stared at the bank president and his associates. "Where's Theron Ware? He was here, where did he go to?"

No one knew, and J. A. Cottrell was indignant.

"Marshal, you don't mean to insinuate that Theron could have taken the money?"

"Figure it out for yourself," Ed Gracey said. "Who else had the opportunity, J. A.?"

Curt didn't know either, but he had a strong hunch where Theron Ware would go.

Theron was aware that Lodestone was to be the point of rendezvous in case the holdup went wrong in any way. Quite likely he also knew that Rita Corday would be there waiting for Jack. There was no more hope for Theron with Lenora Forbes, now that he was a bank robber, but Theron had always wanted Rita, too. With a fortune in his saddlebags, Jack dead, and Curt wounded, Theron might make a final bid for Rita. If Kid Ansted and Dusty Shands showed up, they would be useful as bodyguards on the flight from the Ontawee country. Curt had to catch Theron— and kill him.

"Shut up, damn it!" Ed Gracey said disgustedly to J. A. Cottrell. "There's five men dead in this town, and you're bawling about losing money that don't even belong to you."

SIXTEEN

Rita Corday reached Lodestone well before noon, riding her chestnut mare and leading a packhorse she had bought from Dane Lauritsen at the livery stable. There were some things she couldn't bear to leave behind, although it was necessary to abandon many prized articles of apparel. But her mind was not on this as she rode into the barren ghost town under a gray-clouded gusty sky. She was afraid for Jack Metheny and his comrades. A premonition of disaster and death filled her with cold despair.

Leaving the packhorse in the crumbling shed behind the Silver Cage Opera, Rita drifted about the empty streets in search of the old hermit, Spider Werle, but he was not to be found. He might be dead, she realized with a shudder, and lying somewhere in these ruins. It made the deserted mining camp more eerie than ever, and Rita tried to think of other things.

Last night she had seen Kid Ansted and Dusty Shands, and learned that Curt Metheny was with them now, reunited with his brother. In making the rounds, Dusty and the Kid had stopped at the Mustang, and talked for some time with Rita, whom they knew as Jack's girl. She wondered if Curt was angry at her for concealing Jack's identity all these years. She had often wanted to tell Curt, but Jack had insisted that she keep it a secret. It had been hard though, when she was talking to Curt, and his loneliness was so plain. Rita hoped Curt hadn't joined Utah's crew just in time to die with them, but that would be in keeping with the pattern of the boy's ill-fated life.

Riding the wind-swept street, Rita felt a sudden thrust of pain. It must be ten-thirty, the time set for the holdup. She looked at the tiny jeweled watch Jack had given her, an item of plunder from some old raid. It was ten thirty-five, and all over in Holly, perhaps. She could see them dead in the bank, dead in the street, all of them, and her agony racked her. She could not see them riding clear and free. She tried, but the vision wouldn't come.

If she was wrong, if all went well, they ought to get here around noon, or soon after. But she'd have to wait, if it took all day—and night. She tried in quiet desperation to banish her doubts and fears, to believe in their success and escape. *They'll get here, all right,* she told herself, *and we'll ride out of this country, Jack and Curt and I, into a new and better world.*

In the shed, Rita slid from the saddle, loosened the girth on the chestnut, and crossed the weed-grown yard to the stage door of the old opera hall. In the dim corridor, with dusty boards creaking under her boots, she paused before the door of the dressing room her mother had used, the gilt star faded and frayed on the warped wood. She did not look inside.

On the cluttered stage Rita halted again, beneath the shredded and cobwebbed remnants of the once-gaudy curtains and velvet drapes. Here Selma Corday had sung to packed houses and become the toast of the Ontawee. Men had been shot and killed over her, but Selma had never loved anyone but the man who gave her his name and a daughter, and then vanished forever from her life. Now that daughter stood in the musky shadows and tried to visualize how it must have been when this vast hall was filled with music, lights, and laughter.

Rita shook her coppery head, her green eyes smarting and her throat aching. She looked out over the brass footlamps and orchestra pit to the splintered debris of the main floor, and then up to the great horseshoe of boxes arched above, their drapes filthy and tattered and hanging awry. She descended from the stage and Rita picked her way through dusty litter to the front of the building, eager to get out in the open air once more. This place was too much like a huge tomb.

Outside and breathing in the fresh air, she felt better as she walked aimlessly along the vacant street, past the other legendary landmarks of Lodestone—The Royal Flush, Miners' Rest and The Golden Wheel; Paradise Ballroom and The Highland House.

In the first flush of young love, Rita and Jack Metheny had thought that everything was going to be just the way they wanted it. The wonder of that first flaring passion still set Rita to quivering inside. But it had soon been blighted. The Metheny family was having trouble, going to pieces, and it got so bad Jack couldn't stand it. He ran away to enlist in the cavalry, and left Rita behind. Ever since then she had been waiting, just as she was now, waiting for Jack Metheny. Like Curt and everyone else, Rita supposed he had died with Custer—until that unforgettable night when he had walked into the Mustang with Utah Tyrrell and some other men. Even with that black patch, Rita had known him instantly, and their love had been greater and deeper than ever. They were meant for one another in every way, that was all. Sometimes Rita felt they'd had too much, too early, and that was what they'd had to pay and suffer for later on.

Her watch showed eleven-fifty when she turned back toward the opera house. They should be coming soon now, if nothing had gone wrong. The picture in her mind had changed by this time. They were no longer lying dead in Holly; they were riding free and clear as the wind, riding for Lodestone.

Rita grained and watered the horses and ate a bite from the lunch that she had packed, lunch enough for the whole outfit. By then it was twelve-fifteen, and Rita led the horses to the front of the driveway and left them there. If Utah's bunch was being pursued, they wouldn't want to waste any time here. She doubted the pursuit would be so close, but it was best to be ready.

She sat down to wait on a broken bench in front of the opera hall, but in her anxiety and agitation it was difficult to sit still. Now and then she rose to pace back and forth, pausing occasionally to listen for hoofbeats. Twice she thought she heard horsemen, but each time it was an illusion. By twelve-thirty, she began to fret. They ought to be in Lodestone by now. Something must have happened.

On some impulse she entered the Silver Cage once more and stared around the desolate interior, looking toward the stage this time. Perhaps it was a kind of farewell to her mother, a final look at the scene that had once been dominated by her mother's beauty and talent.

When she returned to the sagging porch, Spider Werle was standing there, a startling apparition at first glance, scarecrow thin in ancient patched buckskins, his white hair long and wild, his white beard soiled and ragged. He carried an old Spencer carbine and peered at the girl with faded, sunken blue eyes.

"If it ain't Miss Selma!" he said, after a moment of study. "My pleasure, ma'am, to welcome you back to Lodestone. The boys'll sure be mighty happy to see you. We was talking about you in the Wheel the other night. Things is kinda slow here right now, ma'am, but they'll pick up again, you bet."

"How've you been, Mr. Werle?" asked Rita kindly.

"Always called me mister. Never would call me Spider. You're a real high-grade lady, Miss Selma. Me? I was kinda poorly for a spell, but I'm coming along good now. Don't tell a soul, but I think I got me a strike up the gulch. Looks like the real bonanza, Miss Selma."

"That's fine, Mr. Werle. I'm glad to hear it."

"This town'll boom again, mark my word," Spider Werle declared solemnly.

"It'll be like the old days, Mr. Werle."

"Like the old days—only better. Bigger and better." The old man stopped and keened the breezy air, head tilted and hand to ear. "Somebody coming."

Rita stepped back inside the gloomy hall, and Spider Werle took his stand at the entrance with carbine ready. The old man always carried that weapon, but had never been known to use it, and most people claimed it wasn't even loaded.

It sounded like a single horseman, Rita realized in dismay, and then her heart went up at the thought that it might be Jack Metheny. The hoofbeats grew closer and louder, and it became evident that there was only one rider coming. Rita shut her tired eyes and prayed for it to be Jack.

Opening her eyes and leaning forward, Rita looked over Spider's bent white head and through the doorway. The rider was in the street now, and coming nearer, moving at last into range of her vision. A tall, dark-clothed man on a bay gelding. But it was not Jack Metheny—it wasn't anyone from the Tyrrell band. It looked like Theron Ware, Rita observed, with a shiver of panic and revulsion. It *was* Theron Ware. *But what is he doing here—alone? What does his coming mean?*

It must mean Theron Ware was Utah's undercover agent in Holly Town. And it could mean, she realized with sick horror, that all the others were dead—or taken prisoners. That Theron Ware was the sole survivor of Utah Tyrrell's outfit.

He must have pulled a doublecross, Rita thought, with acid bitterness. *Theron must have alerted the law and the townspeople, so that the raiders had ridden into another gun trap— another Arrowhead.* Her first vision had been correct: they were all dead in Holly—Well, Theron was going to die for that. Rita Corday herself would kill him, with no regret.

Theron Ware reined up before the opera house, his dark eyes sweeping the length of the street. Under the white hat his handsome features with the nose Curt had broken had a sinister look. Watching him, hand on the short-barreled pistol in her jacket pocket, Rita felt her heart flutter, her throat tighten, and her breath come shallow and uneven. *He knows I'm supposed to meet Jack here,* she thought. *Well, I'll listen to his story first—*

Theron heard and then saw her horses in the drive and smiled as he swung lithely from the saddle.

SEVENTEEN

The temptation of the money had been too much for Theron Ware to resist. The idea had occurred to him when Curt Metheny shot down Bowie Bowden and Herm Goedert, and after old Barney blasted Utah Tyrrell, he knew it would be absurdly easy. J. A. Cottrell was unconscious on the floor, and the clerks, scared witless, were trying to revive him. Barnaby was leaning on the counter, his back to Theron, watching Curt weave toward the front door.

Theron took the moneybags from the vault to the back entryway and left them by the door. His bay horse was outside, saddled and ready for an emergency. Returning quickly to the main room, Theron gun-whipped Barnaby from behind and lowered him to the floor. The clerks hadn't even looked up from Cottrell's sprawled hulk, which they were striving to hoist erect.

For a fleeting instant Theron had a chance to shoot Curt in the back, but he hesitated, wanting that money even more than he wanted Curt's life, and by the time he made up his mind to fire, Curt was gone from view. Theron decided to let him go, then changed his mind again, and lunged through the counter gate toward the entrance. Might as well take Curt and the cash, too.

When he got there, his pistol poised, One-Eyed Jakes had come to a stand between him and Curt, his back toward the bank. Teeth exposed under his mustache, Theron took deliberate aim and shot Jakes between the shoulderblades. He intended to throw another shot at Curt Metheny, but when he saw Curt's gun come up, Theron ducked and ran. It was more important to get out of there with the cash than it was to kill Curt. Or maybe get shot himself.

Barnaby was still down, and the clerks were still crouched intently over their boss. The other three men in the bank were dead. No one noticed Theron Ware as he passed through the foyer and cage and out the back way. He lugged the money outside, stashed it in his saddlebags, mounted the bay gelding, and rode out through back alleys and streets to the eastern outskirts. He was seen, but the observers paid scant attention to him. Everyone was rushing toward Front Street and the bank, where the sound of gunfire had shattered the forenoon quiet.

There was no question in Theron Ware's mind as to his immediate objective. Lodestone was the place of rendezvous, and Rita Corday was waiting there for One-Eyed Jakes and the rest. Theron had the loot, and he would keep the rendezvous. If Ansted and Shands got away and showed up there, Theron could handle them somehow, with his brain if not with a gun. And he prided himself on being a lot better with a gun than most people realized.

It was freakish the way the bank holdup had turned out. Everything was going smooth as silk until the chance appearance of old Barnaby brought about chaos and destruction and the death of at least four men. Theron didn't know how many others might have died in the street. That prank of fate had converted Curt Metheny from an outlaw to a public hero, and transformed Theron Ware from an honored bank official to an outright criminal.

He wondered how much money was riding behind his saddle. There must be at least fifty thousand dollars and possibly more. Enough anyway to make a good start and build a new future somewhere else. Enough to live on the rest of his life, if he handled it properly, and he was experienced and shrewd in financial matters.

It was foolish of me not to kill Curt Metheny, reflected Theron, as he jogged along the grassgrown wagon road. Guess I was too excited and confused. Well, Curt wouldn't go far today with that busted arm. They'd probably put him to bed at Doc Pillon's. And that would give Theron an unobstructed opportunity with Rita Corday. Burning in the saddle at the thought of the beautiful redhead, Theron booted the bay horse into a swifter gait. Rita had scorned and rejected him; now, he would get his revenge. Before he got through with her, Rita would be groveling at his feet.

He had killed the notorious One-Eyed Jakes, but with a shot in the back. There was no satisfaction in that, or in anything—except the fortune crammed into his saddlebags. In that wealth and the conquest of Rita Corday, he would find triumph. But not happiness. There was no such a state for Theron, and he knew it. He was no good. He was a sick man. Theron recognized and admitted this, for the first time, but it only drove him all the harder toward Lodestone and the woman. He could regain some measure of self-respect by conquering her.

Theron rode in warily, scanning the bleached and scoured jumble of ruined buildings. Dusty Shands and Kid Ansted might be here ahead of him, if they had lit out when the shooting started in the bank. Or they might not make Lodestone at all, since Curt must have told them the holdup was a total failure, if he'd seen them outside.

The Silver Cage was the meeting place. Theron drew up in front of it, still searching the dusty street, and heard the nicker and stomp of horses in the alley beside the opera house. Rita's chestnut mare and a pack animal, he saw at a glance, and stepped smiling from his saddle. The swollen clouds above hung low now.

In the entrance Spider Werle was crouched, gripping his rusty carbine, and behind him stood

Rita Corday, straight and full-bodied, lovely even in rough range clothing, her hair glimmering like copper.

"Run along, Spider," said Theron Ware. "I've got business with the lady."

"You ain't going to harm Miss Selma," grumbled the Spider. "You got a look I don't like nor trust, mister man."

Theron laughed and pushed past him to confront the girl.

"What happened at the bank?" Rita Corday asked, with strain in her hushed voice and drawn face.

"Everything went fine," Theron told her. "The others'll be along pretty soon. They had to take a roundabout way."

"You're lying," Rita said flatly.

"Why should I lie to you?"

"You were working with them?"

"I was," Theron said. "Are you as surprised as the rest of Holly Town will be?"

"No, I'm not surprised," Rita said dully. "But I know you're lying."

Theron laughed and moved nearer. "What makes you so sure of that, Rita?"

"I know, I can feel it. They're all dead in Holly—Jack and all of them."

"Jack?" he asked, puzzled. "You mean Jakes? Is he—"

"That's my name for him," Rita said.

"Oh, I see. In memory of Jack Metheny, huh?" Theron smiled slyly.

"You can call it that." Rita's right hand was in her jacket pocket. "Now get out of here."

Still smiling, Theron shook his head. "I'm not going anywhere without you."

"Leave her be, mister," croaked Spider Werle, lining his carbine on Ware. "Miss Selma said git out, so you better git."

Theron whirled, saw the Spencer trained on him, and drew the pistol from his left armpit. Rita's protesting cry was drowned in the roaring gunblast, and Spider Werle went tottering backward, impaled on the leaping flame, to twist and fall in the corner, a scrawny length of sooted buckskin amidst the rubbish.

"You murderer!" Rita Corday said, her face aghast as she yanked at her gun, which had caught in her leather pocket.

Theron Ware wheeled and struck with his left fist as Rita's pistol came clear, catching the side of her jaw and knocking her back against a caved-in table. The weapon flew from Rita's hand, spinning away into the shadows, and Theron holstered his smoking gun and lunged at the girl, lust lighting his eyes and distorting his features.

Half-stunned and severely shaken, Rita Corday writhed off the tilted table top, dodged away from Theron's groping arms, and fled down the aisle toward the stage. Theron Ware took after her, sure of his prey now, mustached upper lip pulled high on his teeth, and something like madness flaring in his dilated black eyes.

He overtook her near the stage and hauled her back off the broken steps into a crushing embrace. Rita tried to fight him off, but Theron kept jolting the heel of his palm into her face, until her senses reeled and dimmed. The first raindrops pelted on the lofty roof and filtered through its gaping holes. Sleeping bats were disturbed on their perches, but the struggling pair below did not hear the patter of rain. Theron Ware had even forgotten the fortune in his saddlebags.

"You were right," he panted. "They're all dead in Holly. Except Curt, and he's wounded. Just you and I, Rita—nobody else."

Her dazed green eyes were so full of loathing that Theron hit her again, using his fist this time, and Rita sagged limp and helpless in his arms.

Lyme Vector, on his way to Holly Town to kill Curt Metheny, was riding through Lodestone when the rain started, and set him to swearing and booting his sorrel along at a faster pace. It was the first time Lyme had ventured out since Saturday night, and the marks Curt had left on him were plainly visible. His eyes were still discolored and puffed, his beaked nose broken and swollen, and there were ragged gaps in his buck teeth. The raw scars on his brow, cheeks, and jaw were there permanently, and Lyme Vector was in a murderous mood. All he lived for now was to see Curt Metheny dead in the dirt at his feet.

The rain came harder, slanting down in wind-torn sheets of silver, and Lyme decided to seek shelter until the initial fury of the storm was spent. Surprised to see three horses huddled beside the old opera house, Lyme headed in there to find refuge. It looked like Theron Ware's big bay gelding, along with the chestnut mare that Rita Corday rode, and a laden packhorse. Lyme Vector swung down, dropped his reins, and ducked for cover. He couldn't figure Theron and Rita being together out here. It was common gossip along the line that Rita despised the young banker, and Lyme didn't know that he blamed her. Lyme had been real tickled when Lenora Forbes broke her engagement to Theron Ware. It was easy to hate Theron.

At the entrance Lyme Vector smelled gun-powder and heard a commotion inside. Stepping into the hall, he glimpsed the shrunken body of old Spider Werle, and then saw the interlocked couple down front by the stage. Theron Ware was with Rita Corday, and she looked either unconscious or dead in his greedy clasp. Lyme Vector strode forward, with a shout:

"Turn that gal loose, Ware!"

Theron dropped Rita with a crash and spun about, his face darkly suffused with passion, his right hand snaking under the lapel of his coat. "Keep out of this, Lyme. She met me here of her own free will."

"She sure lookes it," Lyme Vector jeered.

"Don't meddle in my business, Lyme," warned Theron. "Back out the way you came in. She's nothing to you."

"She's still a woman," Lyme said. "And you're the one that's getting out. Come on now, start moving."

Theron Ware pulled the pistol from the shoulder holster, the barrel just clearing as Lyme Vector drew from the hip with smooth speed. Flame from Lyme's barrel slashed the dimness, and the bullet walloped into Theron's left shoulder, flinging him half-around and throwing his shot wild. Lyme Vector gave him another quick blast, straight through the chest this time, and Theron went lurching back against the stage, a brass footlamp clanging as his head struck it. Theron remembered the money then, the fortune that had been his for such a short space. He could have bought Lyme off.

"You fool," he gasped as he strained to control his jittering gun hand. "All that money—"

Lyme Vector, snarling under his beak of a nose, sent two more slugs home, slamming Theron against the stage. Shattered and sagging there, terror in his eyes and mouth opened in a soundless scream, Theron Ware strove to lift the pistol that had grown too heavy for his hand. The weapon exploded downward, ripping splinters from the planks. Blowing blood in a bright fountain, he heaved upright, teetered forward, took three spraddled steps, and toppled full length on his face in the aisle, with dust fuming up about him. Grimacing, Lyme spat across the man's hunched back.

Lyme Vector reloaded his Colt with automatic deftness and moved on past Ware's body to kneel beside Rita Corday. She was partly conscious, the green eyes coming open in her bruised face.

"It's all right now, Rita," said Lyme, hoarse and gentle. "He's dead. He'll never be no more trouble to you—or anybody."

Lifting her in his great arms, Lyme carried her up the aisle to the front door and out onto the porch. The rain was already slackening as he brought her a canteen to drink from and a blanket to wrap herself in.

"You going to be okay, Rita?" asked Lyme. "I got to be getting on to Holly."

"Can't I ride in with you?" Rita murmured weakly.

"You better rest awhile first," Lyme Vector said. "Nobody else will bother you here. And I've got another man to kill today."

"Not—not Curt Metheny?" She shuddered inside the blanket.

"That's the one, ma'am."

"No, Lyme," whispered Rita. "Curt's already wounded—according to Theron."

"Well, he ain't dead," Lyme Vector said. "And I got to see him dead before I can ever rest again."

With stricken eyes, Rita watched Lyme get into his slicker, mount the raw-boned sorrel, and ride out in the lessening rain. She felt utterly hopeless. Jack was dead, and she had nothing left to live for. She couldn't even feel sorry for Spider Werle. But she might be able to help Jack's kid brother Curt.

Shivering in the blanket, Rita crept reluctantly back into the opera hall to search for her pistol— or Theron Ware's. There was a rifle on Theron's saddle, but she'd never used that type of weapon. Gunsmoke bit at her nostrils and left a foul taste on her tongue. Lyme Vector had saved her from Theron, and she was grateful to him for that. But it wouldn't keep her from shooting Lyme, if she had to, in order to save Curt Metheny's life.

EIGHTEEN

Curt Metheny, his bandaged left arm in a sling, was once more riding the road to Lodestone. Ten years ago he had been following his father Jud along this trace. Today he was on the trail of Theron Ware.

Back in Holly Town, Curt knew, Ed Gracey was gathering a posse, but it would be some time before they got organized to set forth, and they didn't know where to start hunting for Theron anyway. Curt Metheny did. He was positive Theron would head for Lodestone—and Rita Corday.

Ed Gracey had tried to restrict Curt to bed at Doc Pillon's, but Curt had avoided that by promising to go to his own room at the livery barn and take it easy the rest of the day. A white lie, Curt figured, as he bypassed the stable and circled widely toward the Lodestone trail, leaving town like a fugitive instead of the hero he'd become this day.

On Front Street this forenoon, for the first time, men had looked at Curt Metheny with an awed respect that bordered on reverence. He had shown them as he wanted to, but in a different way than he had planned. The same people who had reviled him for years were now singing his praises. They'd known all along that Curt had the right

236

kind of stuff in him. Human nature was a strange thing indeed, Curt mused. The same people who had always lauded Theron Ware were now condemning him without mercy. They'd known all the time, of course, that Theron had a rotten streak under his polished veneer. Well, that's the way people were, and Curt could feel nothing but contempt for humanity at large—contempt and pity.

Curt had aged since breakfast. It showed in his green-gray eyes and marked face. He had killed two men this morning, two outlaws named Bowie Bowden and Herm Goedert, and he was going to kill again. He might have suffered some remorse, if his brother Jack and Utah Tyrrell hadn't died, too. The loss of that pair, and Jack in particular, numbed Curt against all other emotions. The only objective he had left was to get Theron Ware, and before Theron could harm Rita Corday. Nothing else seemed to matter, not even Lenora Forbes now that his brother was dead.

The motion of the horse sent pain lancing through Curt's wounded arm, but it wasn't too bad. In fact, it helped keep his senses honed sharp and keen. Overhead the clouds were darkening, and the wind that whipped the treetops had the smell and feel of rain in it. Grazing cattle were huddled together, and gophers, prairie dogs and jack-rabbits were scuttling for cover. The cry of curlews sounded lonely across the dun plains, occasionally broken by the chatter of magpies. Above the alders of the Little Ontawee, king-fishers and mergansers swooped in lazy watchful arcs, now and then plunging downward at the stream.

Curt wondered where Kid Ansted and Dusty Shands were by this time, and hoped again they would get away clean and safe. There was no loot for them to share, unless they went to Lodestone and collected it from Theron Ware, but at least they were alive and unhurt. With the start they had, Dusty and the Kid ought to breeze out of the Ontawee country with something to spare.

He kicked the big gray into a high lope, in an attempt to cut down the lead Theron had attained. With this horse under him, Curt was certain of catching Theron sooner or later, but he wanted it to be in time for Rita Corday. The vision of Jack's girl struggling in the arms of Theron filled him with fury and hate.

Monday noon, Curt thought in wonder. Just a week ago today I was out looking for a riding job, hitting one ranch after another, getting turned down everywhere I went. It seemed incredible that so much could have happened in one week. The sequence of events flickered through Curt's mind, vivid and fleeting. The brushoff at Frying Pan and the argument with Harry Keech. Finding Lenora Forbes at the

South Waterhole, and battling there with Theron Ware and Lyme Vector. The meeting that night with Rita Corday in Lodestone, and the verbal duel with Stan Russett.

Then back to the livery stable routine in Holly, talking with Dane Lauritsen and Tee Dee and Barnaby, and reliving that nightmare of ten years back. An evening at the river side with Lenora Forbes, another clash with Russett, and the shooting match out behind the Mustang, Curt and Barney against Theron Ware, to spring clear One-Eyed Jakes, the bandit they didn't know was Curt's brother Jack. The savage brawl with Alvah Parkhurst in the livery barn, and the bitter aftermath in which Curt was completely ostracized and threatened with lynching.

That brought it up to Saturday night, the fight with Lyme Vector in the Ten-High Saloon, the ruckus at the town-hall dance, and the pistol-whipping by Stan Russett, which Curt later repaid in kind. The coming of Utah Tyrrell's band, the strange and wonderful reunion with his brother Jack, and the ride out toward the Sand Hills. Sunday in camp and the burial of Old Pitts, last night back in town to say his farewells, and then this morning the bank job.

All that in a week's time. It was beyond comprehension and belief. A week of facing death, topped off by a day of dealing it out. Theron Ware would be the sixth man to die, as soon as Curt caught up with him. Theron was an evil to be blasted out of existence, and Curt Metheny had to do the blasting.

The wounded arm made Curt forget his minor hurts, the starched soreness of his face and hands, the painful knot on his skull. He marveled again at the way Utah Tyrrell had held his fire. If Utah had been willing to kill Curt, he could have shot his way out of the bank and ridden off with the Kid and Dusty.

But Utah hadn't seemed to care much, one way or another. It was almost as if he welcomed death. Utah hadn't tried very hard to fire back at old Barney. And Jack Metheny could have escaped alive too if he hadn't stopped to talk with Curt. The bullet Jack had taken in the back, from Theron Ware's pistol, was the one Theron had meant for Curt.

Craving tobacco, Curt looped his reins on the horn, fished a plug out of a vest pocket, and bit off a good chew. With that arm in a sling everything he did seemed awkward and unbalanced. When the time came to fight, Curt would unsling the bandaged arm and let it hang free—if useless. It wasn't wise to underestimate Theron Ware. For all of his flaws and faults, Theron could fight when he had to, with either his fists or a gun.

The clouds hung black and low now, and the gusty air was damp and raw. Lightning flashed along the western horizon, and thunder muttered

240

and rumbled in the distant mountains. Curt untied his slicker and draped it capelike over his shoulders, buttoned at the neck. The first large drops of moisture fell splashing, and then the rain came sweeping down on the rolling plains, turning the reddish-brown earth dark and glistening. Head bent into the storm, Curt cursed and spat tobacco juice and watched the sleek gray hide of the horse blacken and shine wetly. After the first heavy downpour, the rain slowed to a light, steady spatter.

Approaching the Parkhurst spread, Curt felt the familiar chill and nausea, but not as strong as in the past. A new tragedy had partly obliterated the old one. His narrow stare shifted from the dugout to the cottonwood grove, where a kid of fifteen had sat his horse and watched his father walk casually forward into a rifle muzzle. Curt saw and heard it all again: the guns blasting and roaring within the logs, and then smoke floating out from an awful stillness into the dusk. *Dad never killed Ma,* he thought now, as he had then. *I know damn well he didn't.*

Curt was wondering how much those trees had grown in ten years, when he saw a tall rider on a sorrel horse come out of the dripping cotton-woods to block the trail ahead of him. Lyme Vector, uglier than ever with his beak broken, his teeth jagged, and a murderous hatred in his pale eyes. *What a hell of a time for Lyme to pop up,*

Curt thought, in angered annoyance. *It's not him I want; it's Theron Ware.*

Lyme gigged his sorrel forward at a walk, and Curt urged the gray on to meet him. The rain was fading into a sort of sifting mist. It felt like cold sweat on Curt's cheeks, and the slow trickle from his armpits was even colder.

"Don't get in my way today, Lyme," called Curt Metheny. "I've got something to do, and it can't wait."

"You ain't going nowhere from here, Metheny!" yelled Lyme Vector, his craggy dark features convulsed. "This is the end of the road for you, boy."

"Some other time." Curt was impatient and irritable. "I've got to get to Lodestone."

"There ain't no hurry. I just come from there." Lyme laughed like a barking coyote. "It's deader'n ever, Curt."

"You see anybody there, Lyme?"

"Maybe—maybe not. It don't matter none to you."

"It matters plenty," Curt said grimly. "Don't try to hold me up here. I've got business ahead."

"You're held up as of now, stableboy. You got business with me right here."

"I haven't got time to fool around, damn it," Curt said. "Don't try to stop me, Lyme."

"You're stopped, boy, and this ain't fooling," Lyme Vector said. "This is dead-serious and for all the marbles. Climb off that horse, Curt, and we'll do it right—this time."

They had halted as if in common accord, perhaps ninety feet apart, eyeing one another through the thin misty rain that seeped into the muddy ruts between them. Curt smelled wet grass and mulch and sage brush as the big gray stirred restlessly beneath him. There was a cold flutter of panic under his breastbone, and icy needles prickled the length of his spinal column. This wasn't going the way it should. The appearance of Lyme Vector had thrown everything out of kilter.

"I've got no more quarrel with you, Lyme," he said evenly. "That fight in the Ten-High was enough for me."

"But not for me!" Lyme Vector grated. "I don't take a licking like that without coming back. If I couldn't do it with my hands, I'll do it, by God, with a gun."

Curt shook his head, and water flirted from his hatbrim. "This don't call for shooting, Lyme."

"It calls for just that and nothing else," Lyme declared. "Get down and we'll have it, fair and square."

Curt slipped his left arm out of the sling, under the shawled slicker, and let the left palm rest on his thigh, feeling the long muscles twitch and quiver beneath it. "I'm after a man I've got to kill, Lyme. Let me get him first, for Godsake."

"Who is it?"

"Theron Ware."

Lyme Vector's great shoulders shook with laughter, his vulture-like head tossing in morbid glee. "I done the job for you, boy. Theron Ware's laying dead in the Silver Cage. I just killed him there."

Feeling stunned and cheated, Curt Metheny stared at the towering rider. "Is that the truth, Lyme? Honest to God? It is, for a fact? Damn you, I wanted him myself."

"Take me instead," Lyme said, with a gap-toothed grin. "I'm more of a match for you, kid."

"I haven't got that feeling—against you." It was true. Curt had been set on killing Theron, and with Theron dead he had no more incentive to fight. He felt drained empty.

"Better work up some feeling, boy," said Lyme Vector. "Because I'm going to shoot the guts outa you, whether you lift a gun or not."

"Is Rita Corday all right?" Curt inquired, as if he hadn't heard what Lyme said at all.

"Yeah, I got there just about in time—for her. But not for poor old Spider Werle. He was dead when I come in. Theron shot him. So come on now, Curt, let's get to it. Quit stalling and face up to it like a man. Off that horse, boy." Lyme shrugged out of his slicker and let it fall back over the cantle.

Sighing wearily, Curt Metheny undid the top

buttons and shucked off the draped raincoat. He had no heart for this encounter. The keen fighting edge was blunted. But there was no way out of it that he could figure. He had to kill Lyme Vector or die himself.

"We won't draw till we're on the ground and both ready," Lyme said. "Step down when I do, boy. It's fitting that you get it here, where your mammy got it. And your pappy lit out on his last ride."

"All right, you buzzard," Curt gritted. "You want it that bad, I'll give it to you for sure."

They dismounted in slow, careful unison, watching each other with slit-eyed closeness, and Curt was a trifle clumsy on account of the crippled left arm. He was grateful for the flare of temper that Lyme's last speech had stirred up in him.

"Who winged you, Curt?" asked Lyme, drying his hands under his denim jacket.

"Utah Tyrrell."

"And you killed Utah, I suppose?" Lyme said jeeringly.

"No, but Barney did." The chewing tobacco was dry in Curt's mouth.

"Well, I'll be damned. And who did you get?"

"Bowden and Goedert," said Curt, wiping his right hand on his shirt.

"Now ain't that something?" laughed Lyme Vector. "Downing you ought to give me quite a rep, huh?"

They moved aside from their horses, tracking mud into the wet brown grass, and paced toward one another until the distance was shortened to about fifty feet. The grass swished under Curt's boots and snarled in his spur rowels. He noticed a clump of sage behind Vector that shone like tarnished silver in the rain. His tongue felt leathery, and his throat was dry and tight.

At a standstill now, they waited and measured each other with cold, deadly intentness, keying themselves toward the fateful moment of striking.

"This has been a long time coming," Lyme Vector said, his splintered fangs bared beneath the crooked beak of a nose. "But you're going to die now!"

"You're some talker, Lyme," said Curt. "Let's see how you shoot."

At that instant, as they hovered on the hair-trigger edge of drawing, Curt glimpsed movement in the road beyond Vector's sorrel, and let his glance stray in that direction long enough to identify Rita Corday on her chestnut, leading two other horses. Curt's green eyes flicked back to Vector, and his right hand streaked to his gun, but Lyme had seen his chance and started his motion in that split-second when Curt had been distracted. That was all it took in a gun fight.

Curt knew he was late, even before fire bloomed bright-red from Lyme's rising barrel, and something smashed into Curt's body with the force of a sledge hammer, beating him backward with his heels gouging the dirt. Curt had been firing when he was hit, and his first shot had missed, thrown off by the jarring impact of Lyme's bullet.

Regaining his balance and lunging forward into a spread-legged crouch, Curt lined another shot into the muzzle light that burst toward him as the Colt sprang hard in his hand. Through the stabbing gun-flames, Curt saw water spurt from Lyme's left shoulder and the denim jacket go dark with blood, as his slug spun the big man into a reeling half-turn.

Vector had missed with his second shot, the whiplash wind of it fanning past Metheny's ear, but something had burst wide open inside of Curt, flooding his body with scalding agony. His eyes blurred and went blind, his breath caught and gagged in his throat, and he could no longer control the .44 in his right hand. He spat out the tobacco cud, strangely reddened, and he wanted to scream out in protest "No, no, I wasn't ready, this isn't fair—" But no words came. His lungs were filling up with liquid, and the earth was dipping and rocking crazily under his boots.

Lyme Vector's gun was ablaze again, torching away at Curt through a smoky, shimmering haze. Lead tugged at Curt's clothes and seared his skin, the concussions dinning in his numbed brain, until another wicked blast shocked him backward. The ground slammed against his shoulderblades as the world was blown bottom-side up and shattered into fiery fragments.

Then Curt Metheny was lying on his back in the wet grass, arms and legs stretched slackly asprawl, his eyes dimming, his head aching hollowly, and that scalding pain swelling within him. He tasted blood and grit and gunsmoke in his mouth, and the odor of raw earth and damp grass came to him, faintly spiced with sage. He was dying. He could feel life ebbing out of him, seeping into the rain-soaked soil. He had looked away from his man and down the road for a fractional second, and that had killed him—with Lyme Vector's help.

There would be no ranch to work with Barney and Tee Dee, no home for Rita—and maybe for Lenora Forbes, as his wife. There would be nothing. He was dying, and he longed to call out to Jack and Utah, *"Wait for me, wait! I'm coming too. I'm coming with you—"* But no sound came from him except a strangled sob.

The last thing Curt Metheny saw was sparkling grasstops against a darkening sky. The last thing he felt was the slow, cool filter of rain on his face.

Rita Corday, the lead ropes cast off behind her, was riding toward Lyme Vector, pistol in hand, death on her fine bruised features. Lyme couldn't shoot a woman, and he didn't want to be shot by one either. He flung himself into his saddle, whirled the sorrel about, and set off at a racking gallop.

Rita Corday threw a few futile long-range shots after Lyme, and then gave it up. She had come too late. Only by a couple of minutes or so, but that was late enough. It seemed like the end of the world to her. There was nothing left to live for.

Leaving the horses in the muddy roadway, Rita went to kneel in the grass at the side of Curt Metheny, her bare, coppery head jeweled with mist. The gun was still gripped in Curt's right hand, and raindrops glittered on his lean, scarred face. Rita bent and kissed the dead mouth, and her tears mingled with the rain on his cheeks.

Around Holly Town and all over the Ontawee country, they were talking about Curt Metheny.

In the streets and backyards, the homes and stores, the saloons and hash houses, the gambling halls and poolrooms, from the Mustang down the line, everyone was talking about Curt Metheny, with pride and pleasure as well as sorrow in their voices.

Out on the range it was the same, in every ranch-house and line camp and bunkhouse, every dugout and soddy; and around the corrals and feed pens and blacksmith shops, the barns, sheds, and yards, the chuck wagons and open cookfires. They were telling the story of Curt Metheny, dead in his prime at twenty-five, and only because that skunk of a Lyme Vector had got the drop and taken Curt by surprise. Lyme couldn't have done it any other way.

Five dead men in Holly, and three dead men in Lodestone. Curt was one of them, and he had killed only two of the others, but he was the hero, the boy who had busted up the Tyrrell bunch. A legend that would grow and spread and live forever in the West.

"Sure, he was a fighter and a great one," they said. "He come by it natural enough, too. His father before him was a great fighting man. Hellfire and lightning in any kind of a battle, that was old Judson Metheny. And young Curt Metheny was the same way. It was in his blood, birthed right in the boy, burnt deep in his brain and heart, in his blood and bones.

"A real great one, and no mistake. They don't come any better. . . . Always knew he had it in him. You can tell the real ones. . . . The look of an eagle in his eyes, the lines of a thoroughbred on him, and moving quick and easy as a mountain cat.

"Fighting men like Curt Metheny are born—not made."

"—and there's one thing that would please Curt a whole lot," old Barnaby told Dane Lauritsen and Tee Dee in the livery barn. "What he done today went a long way toward clearing the name of his father—and the whole Metheny family. Not that they ever needed clearing, in my way of thinking."

"Curt was the best," said little Tee Dee, his smile brave and proud through a sheen of tears. "There'll never be another like him."

Dane Lauritsen, his own eyes misted and red, nodded solemnly, swallowed hard, and bit down again on the cold mangled cigar.

Roe Richmond was born Roaldus Frederick Richmond in Barton, Vermont. Following graduation from the University of Michigan in 1933, Richmond found jobs scarce and turned to writing sports stories for the magazine market. In the 1930s he played semi-professional baseball and worked as a sports editor on a newspaper. After the Second World War, Richmond turned to Western fiction and his name was frequently showcased on such magazines as *Star Western*, *Dime Western*, and *Max Brand's Western Magazine*. His first Western novel, *Conestoga Cowboy*, was published in 1949. As a Western writer, Richmond's career falls into two periods. In the 1950s, Richmond published ten Western novels and among these are his most notable work, *Mojave Guns* (1952), *Death Rides the Dondrino* (1954), *Wyoming Way* (1958), and in 1961 *The Wild Breed*. Nearly an eighteen-year hiatus followed during which Richmond worked as copy editor and proofreader for a typesetting company. Following his retirement, he resumed writing. Greg Tobin, an editor at Belmont Tower, encouraged Richmond to create the Lash Lashtrow Western series. In these original paperback novels, Richmond was accustomed to go back and rework short novels about Jim

Hatfield that he had written for *Texas Rangers* magazine in the 1950s. When Tobin became an editor at Bantam Books, he reprinted most of Richmond's early novels in paperback and a collection of his magazine fiction, *Hang Your Guns High!* (1987). Richmond's Western fiction is notable for his awareness of human sexuality in the lives of his characters and there is a gritty realism to his portraits of frontier life.